Darkest Before the Dawn

Darkest Before the Dawn

Gwen Kirkwood

ROBERT HALE · LONDON

© Gwen Kirkwood 2013
First published in Great Britain 2013

ISBN 978 0 7198 0929 3

Robert Hale Limited
Clerkenwell House
Clerkenwell Green
London EC1R 0HT

www.halebooks.com

The right of Gwen Kirkwood to be identified as author
of this work has been asserted by her in accordance with the
Copyright, Designs and Patents Act 1988

2 4 6 8 10 9 7 5 3 1

Typeset in Bookman Old style
Printed by MPG Printgroup, UK

ACKNOWLEDGEMENTS

My thanks to Dumfries & Galloway Constabulary for explaining the procedures and diligence involved during and after a serious road accident, particularly regarding the care of the victims and the need to establish their correct identities, and to contact their relatives with sensitivity and understanding.

I would also like to express my sincere appreciation to Francis and Jacquie McFaul for their frank discussion following a leg amputation: the personal anguish, the physical, life-changing difficulties, and the need for love, patience and support from those nearest and dearest, whose lives are also affected.

ONE

Rosemary Caraford felt a shiver of apprehension at the sight of the blue lights of a police car drawing up at her door. Why should she feel this peculiar premonition of disaster tonight? Normally she was a practical, level-headed woman and she would be the first to admit it was ridiculous to feel any sort of alarm. The police were only doing their job, and they often needed to come to the farm to report a minor road accident which had demolished part of a fence, especially when there were animals in the field which might stray onto the road and cause another accident. Sometimes they came to enquire about the tenants in one of the cottages – all perfectly simple explanations. She straightened her shoulders, opened the door and looked questioningly at the two police officers, summoning her usual ready smile despite her exhaustion after a hard day's work. In spite of her resolve to be calm and sensible, her heart raced at their first question.

'Yes, this is Martinwold Farm.' She could feel

the colour ebbing from her face. 'William Alexander Caraford? Yes, this is his address. Billy is our son.' She was an intelligent and capable woman but right now her brain seemed to be turning to mush. She couldn't remember the registration number of Billy's car. Why did the police need it, or Billy? She stared at Sergeant Gregory and Police Constable Hazel Jacobs. She was too agitated by their presence and their carefully worded questions to think clearly. It had been a long day, but a satisfying one, beginning with the good news brought by Jim Atkins, the postie, who had arrived while they were still finishing breakfast.

It was a sunny August morning and the postman was whistling happily when he arrived at Martinwold Farm. Billy jumped to his feet, his breakfast forgotten. Tension and excitement warred with each other over his lean young face. This was the day for the exam results. All he'd ever wanted to do was follow in his father's footsteps and farm but he knew farming needed some education these days if he was to keep up with modern trends and all the regulations which kept pouring in from Brussels. In any case, he had been brought up to make the most of his abilities and opportunities. At seventeen that meant concentrating on his schoolwork.

'You're early this morning, Jim,' Sam Caraford greeted the postman with a smile.

'Aye, the young folk are all waiting impatiently for these.' He pointed to the large brown envelope on top of the pile and grinned across at Billy, already stretching out a hand for the letter.

'Sure you don't want me to open it?' his father teased.

'Not on your life,' Billy said, ripping open the envelope, holding his breath. 'Yes! Yes!' he yelled seconds later. 'I've passed! I've passed them all! They're all A grades, even my French.'

'We never doubted you'd pass them, did we, Sam?' his mother said, beaming with pride.

'Aye, it pays to work hard.' The elderly postman nodded. 'But ye're a clever laddie anyway. So is your pal, Liam, up at Highfold. I've just come from there. He said I could tell you he has passed all his exams too and he's looking forward to meeting up for a celebration at Gino's tonight. He's a grand laddie, young Liam. He's ten times the lad o' that wastrel half-brother o' his. All Derek Lennox and his gang care about is drinking. Drugs as weel if the rumours be true, but his father willna hear a word against him, not even after he lost his driving licence and then took his brand new Range Rover without permission and crashed it.'

'You don't really think Derek takes drugs, do you, Jim?' Rosemary asked anxiously. 'Surely there's not many people take drugs in a country area like this?'

'There may not be as many as in the city, but from what I hear there's a fair few, and Derek Lennox and his gang are amongst 'em. He's breaking Mrs Lennox's heart, so he is.' He sighed heavily.

'Yes, so I believe,' Rosemary said. 'Jane has always done her best to treat him the same as Liam and Fenella, her own two children, but since Derek reached his teens she says he resents all her efforts to be a good mother to him. I know she has a struggle trying to guide him. It's a pity his own father doesn't give his support.'

'Young Derek threw away his own opportunities as soon as he started secondary school and got in with a gang. He didn't pass any exams and I reckon he's jealous o' young Liam now,' Jim Aitken said, shaking his grey head. 'Young folk have great opportunities these days. It's good to see some of ye making the most o' them, Billy. I wish you, and young Liam, the best o' luck, laddie. He's hoping ye'll phone him as soon as ye've opened your results. Young Fenella has done well too. She tells me she wants to be a vet. It looks like she'll be following the pair o' ye to university in another couple o' years.'

'Thanks, Jim.' Billy grinned at him. 'I'll phone Highfold right away.' The old postman nodded. He enjoyed his job. He knew the affairs of most of the country folk and he shared their joys and their sorrows, but there were changes ahead and he was hoping they wouldn't come before he was ready to retire.

'I can see there'll be a crowd at Gino's tonight,' his father said when the postman had gone, whistling on his way. Sam knew the young folk gathered at the coffee shop in town when they had anything to celebrate. The owner, a second-generation Italian, always made them welcome so long as they didn't get too rowdy.

'I'll phone Liam,' Billy said. 'I knew he would do brilliantly. He's set his heart on a career in medical research. He can't wait to get away from Derek's scorn. Even Mr Lennox disapproves of him planning to spend years at university.'

'Derek Lennox is probably wishing he'd worked harder himself when he had the chance, instead of bunking off with his friends at every opportunity,' Rosemary said.

'I don't know what he thinks,' Billy said, his young face troubled, 'but he's in with a really bad crowd. Liam says his mother is worried sick but Derek's father refuses to listen to any criticism so long as Derek plans to follow in his footsteps and take over the tenancy of Highfold. The trouble is, he's hardly ever there, and when he is, Liam says he's not fit to work. It's Liam who has done most of the extra work at the silage and harvest this summer, even though he has no desire to farm. He feels it's his duty to help his stepfather and work for his keep.'

'Yes, the vet was saying the same thing when he was here the other day,' Sam said. 'He had been doing the TB testing at Highfold and he said it was Liam who had all the ear numbers and records sorted in readiness. Syd Lennox will miss him more than he realizes when he goes to university. It needs more than brawn these days to keep up with things.'

'I'll go and phone Liam now,' Billy said, 'but celebrations at Gino's will have to wait until tomorrow night. The contractor wants to finish combining the Langlee field by tonight. Here's hoping we don't have any breakdowns.'

'Och, I reckon we shall manage if we get a good start,' his father said. 'We'll excuse you from working late in the field if you deal with the milking?'

'Oh yes, I can do that OK,' Billy said eagerly. He loved all the farm work and the changing seasons, but most of all he enjoyed working with the dairy herd.

'Your mother and I are proud of you, son. You deserve a wee celebration with your friends. Anyway, we shall have to get used to managing without you when you go away to university.'

'We–ell, if you're sure.' Billy didn't like leaving any job unfinished. 'It's true most of our friends will be at Gino's tonight, even if some of them have not got the grades they hoped for. Will you be able to give Liam and me a lift into town then, Mum?'

'I reckon we can do better than a lift, can't we, Rosie?' Sam looked across at his wife with a conspiratorial smile. 'You'll be eighteen next month. You've been driving tractors since you could reach the pedals and it's nearly a year since you passed your driving test. We know you're steady, so we've bought you a wee car of your own. It's not a new one, mind you,' Sam warned, 'but it's in good condition. It's only had one owner, an elderly lady, so it hasn't done a big mileage. We've registered and insured it in your own name but the rest will be up to you. That should be enough to make you go carefully, eh?'

'A car of my own?' Billy echoed, his blue eyes shining. 'Really?' He turned to look at his mother. She smiled back at him.

'It was to be for your birthday but Willie Blake knew the previous owner and he said it was a bargain. It's been ready to drive away for the past month, but Willie agreed to keep it at the garage. You've worked hard, Billy, and we were sure you'd do well in your exams. Anyway, your father has an ulterior motive, haven't you, Sam?'

'Oh aye.' Sam grinned at them both. 'We thought if you have your own wheels you'll be able to come home for the weekend once a month and do the relief milking.'

'That's brilliant,' Billy said. 'I'll come every fort-night and keep to my present routine, doing the relief milking every second weekend as I've done for the past two years. I've been saving up and I'll need to keep on earning money when I'm living away from home.'

'And buying your own petrol, as well as toothpaste and shampoo!' his mother teased.

'My own car? I can't believe it!' He seized his mother in a bear hug, lifting her off her chair. Rosemary Caraford was small and neat and Billy was even taller than his father now.

'Put me down! Behave yourself,' she squeaked, shaking her head and laughing. 'You were such a puny wee thing. How you ever grew so big and strong I don't know.'

'Will you run him into the garage to pick up the car, Rosie?' Sam asked. 'It's a silver Vauxhall Astra, Billy.'

'I don't care what make it is so long as it goes and I can be independent,' Billy said happily. 'To be honest, that was the worst bit about going away to university, not being able to get home regularly and see what was going on with the cows and the farm. Now everything will be perfect.' He grinned and hugged his mother again, then turned to Sam. 'Thanks, Dad,' he said a little gruffly. Sam slapped him on the back.

'You're a good laddie. We shall miss you when you go away.'

The milking was finished, the parlour all washed up, ready for the morning milking, and the cows had been taken back to their pasture for the night. It was a lovely summer evening. Billy dashed up to the house to grab a sandwich and a cup of tea before he collected Liam and his sister. Fenella was meeting her own friends at Gino's and she had asked for a lift when she heard Billy had got a car of his own. Their mothers had taken turns at chauffeuring their offspring to various school or sports functions ever since the two boys started primary school. They would be independent now, Billy thought happily. They were neighbouring farmers and the two families got on well – or at least they had until about two years ago when Derek Lennox had appeared in court on a charge of dangerous driving.

He had run into the car of a middle-aged couple before knocking down a long length of fencing and ending up in one of the Martinwold fields. Although there were animals grazing in the field he had left his vehicle and run home without reporting the accident. Fortunately the driver of a van had seen the crash and stopped to help the couple in the other car. They had reported the accident to the police but Samuel Caraford had been called as a witness to corroborate the police report concerning the broken fencing and the car abandoned in his field. Since then Mr Lennox had barely spoken to any of the Carafords.

'It isn't just your family,' Liam had said to Billy apologetically. 'My dad is making life hell for Fenella and me, and we think it's even worse for my mother. She's moved into the spare bedroom but she still tries to humour him. It makes me furious inside when he ignores her. She looks so unhappy. He keeps muttering about the time I spend at school and doing my homework. He wants me to leave school and work on the farm, but I'd only be running after him and

Derek, and he knows I've always wanted a career in medical research. You'd think he would understand when my real dad was a doctor.' Billy listened and agreed with his friend, knowing talking to him was Liam's way of dealing with the increasing stress at home. Derek had missed school at every opportunity and left as soon as he could, without qualifications or ambition to do anything except enjoy life.

'It's not worth arguing with either my dad or Derek,' Liam told Billy bitterly one day after he had allowed Derek to provoke him. 'I told him any career was better than throwing my life away on drink and drugs as he was doing. I reminded him that he's never fit to drive machinery before midday.' Liam had arrived at school with a black eye and a bruised cheek. The man he regarded as his father had struck him. It was a shock. The blow had made him aware of his real place in the Lennox family. He and his sister only bore Syd Lennox's name because he had adopted them when he had married their mother, but Derek bore his father's blood as well as his name. As a doctor their own father had died while struggling to save the lives of fellow passengers during a train crash. His mother had been expecting Fenella at the time and Liam had been two years old. They had moved to live at his grandparents' farm and Fenella had been born three months later.

'My mum had known the Lennox family for years,' Liam once told Billy. 'She had been at school with the first Mrs Lennox. Fenella and I had no dad and Derek had no mum so I suppose marriage was a convenient solution.' Billy did not miss the undertone of bitterness in his voice. 'We've always regarded him as our dad,' Liam went on. 'He has been good to us until recently. Since Derek left school and Fenella and I have made our own choices to aim at university, his attitude has changed.'

'I expect it's hard for him to see his own son making such a mess of life, when you and Fenella are working hard and doing so well at school,' Billy replied, subconsciously quoting his own mother, but the episode had strengthened Liam's determination to do well at school and get away to university at the first opportunity.

'If Derek wants to throw his life away then let him get on with it. I intend to make a life for myself. If I can do some good for other folks along the way then that will be a bonus. Fenella wants to be a vet. Mum says she has enough money set aside from our grandfather's legacy to help both of us with university expenses, so we won't be depriving Derek of anything.'

As he drove to Highfold, Billy was thinking about these things and feeling happy that his friend would now be able to embark on the career he had dreamed of. Both Fenella and Liam were ready and waiting when he arrived and Mrs Lennox came to the door with them to admire his car and to congratulate him warmly on his exam results. He could see how proud and happy she was that Liam and Fenella had done so well.

'I must congratulate you too, Billy. You'll be Doctor Caraford, Minister of Agriculture, before we know where we are,' she teased.

He grinned back at her.

'There's no fear of that. All I want is my degree in agriculture to keep the teachers and my parents satisfied, then I intend to get on with farming and breeding even better cows than my father, and my Uncle Alex at Bengairney.' He was smiling but deep down he knew this was his secret ambition. His father and grandfather and generations before them had been farmers and good stockmen so he considered himself a true son of the soil.

Most of their friends were already gathered at Gino's when Billy parked carefully in an empty space on the side of the street a few yards away from the door. Inside the coffee bar everyone was in high spirits, even those who had not achieved the grades they had hoped for. Someone had already put the music on and Gino himself was smiling widely. He knew many of the youngsters by name and he welcomed their trade and their youthful spirits and optimism. He was a tolerant, jovial little man but he was quick to sense troublemakers and recently there had been one or two he had banned from his premises.

They had been in the coffee bar a couple of hours when Fenella and two of her friends moved to the table where Liam and Billy and their friends were making the most of the evening breeze from the open door. There were bench seats on either side and some of the boys made room for the girls to squeeze in beside them. Liam and Billy had unzipped their fleeces and laid them on the bench between them. The girls had their cardigans loosely draped around their shoulders as they sipped the long cool fruit drinks which Gino made with such flare. They were all laughing at a joke told by one of Liam's pals when Fenella looked up at the sound of a familiar guffaw coming from the pavement outside. Her brother Derek and some of his friends were walking around Billy's car, trying the doors, peering inside, pulling the windscreen wipers and pinging them back. She tensed.

'Here comes trouble,' she said in a low voice, stretching one leg beneath the table to give Liam a gentle kick and get his attention. 'Derek and a couple of his friends are coming in.'

'They can't. Gino has banned them.'

'They're behind you,' she mouthed silently.

'Billy, I think we should leave,' Liam muttered, getting to his feet. 'Derek has been in a foul mood and spoiling for trouble all day.'

'OK, suits me. We've a busy day's harvesting tomorrow anyway so I promised we wouldn't be too late home.' Billy stretched backwards to get the car key from the front pocket of his slim-fitting jeans.

'Hey, brainbox! Watch where you're putting that big head o' yours,' a voice growled as Billy hooked the key with his forefinger and drew it out.

'Sorry. Didn't know you were standing behind me, Derek,' Billy said amiably, as he tried to get to his feet in the narrow space. Quick as lightning, Derek snatched the car key while Billy was balanced on one leg, extricating himself from the bench seat.

'Hey, give me my key!' he yelled but Derek was already running out to the car, clicking to unlock the door. Liam was suddenly standing, anxious to leave without a quarrel. He ran after Derek, with Billy in hot pursuit.

Fenella stood up, intending to leave with the boys. She ran round the table but by the time she reached the door of the coffee bar Derek was already in the driver's seat of Billy's car, revving up the engine. Liam jumped into the passenger seat, trying to reason with his brother but Derek lashed out with his fist, knocking his head against the window. Billy paused for an instant, staring in anger and dismay, then he ran forward, just in time to jump into the back seat before Derek shot into the line of traffic and zoomed down the main street amidst a blare of horns from angry drivers travelling in both directions. Fenella clapped a hand to her mouth to stifle a scream as she and her friend, Amanda, watched from the door of Gino's.

'Don't worry, Fen. They'll not go far. Billy will be back for you in no time. He and Liam have both left their jackets behind.'

'So they have. I'd better get them,' Fenella said, still staring after the car. 'I'll bet they've left their phones in them. I'll—' She gasped aloud when the car shot through the traffic lights at red further down the street, then swerved to the right across the line of oncoming traffic. Her stomach lurched. 'Derek is driving like a maniac. He has no licence and he's heading out of town.'

'He and his pals have been drinking again. You could smell it as soon as they came in,' Amanda said in a low voice, her own concern increasing. She had a teenage crush on Liam. 'I didn't think he'd really drive away.'

TWO

Back at Martinwold, Rosemary did her best to answer Sergeant Gregory's questions.

'Y–yes, I think that is the correct registration. It's a silver Vauxhall Astra. W–we only collected it from the garage this morning.' Please God don't let anything have happened to Billy, she prayed silently, staring wide-eyed at the police sergeant. She thought she saw sympathy on his lined face and her stomach muscles clenched. She clutched the edge of the door for support.

'May we come in, Mrs Caraford?' PC Hazel Jacobs asked gently, stepping forward and taking her arm.

'Y–yes, yes, of course.'

'Is there anyone else here? Staying in the house with you?' Sergeant Gregory asked.

'My husband is here. H–he has just gone up to bed. It will be another busy day at the harvest tomorrow.' She was beginning to shiver.

'I suggest you ask him to join us, if you don't mind, Mrs Caraford?' Sergeant Gregory's voice was kind but

Rosemary knew it was more of a command than a request.

'Is Billy in some sort of trouble? Was he talking on his mobile? Surely he wasn't speeding? I know he would never drink and drive so it can't be that. He hardly drinks alcohol at all, thank goodness. What—'

'We shall try to answer your questions, Mrs Caraford, if you will ask your husband to join us. Please?' Sergeant Gregory interrupted, knowing it was probably nerves and apprehension making her chatter.

'Y–yes. Of course. Will you go through to the room?' Rosemary waved a hand towards a half-open door. Although she was almost fifty her hair was still blonde and as curly as it had always been. She shook it now like a confused child trying, and failing, to understand her lessons. 'Take a seat. I'll tell Sam to get dressed and come downstairs again.'

She went towards the staircase but Sam was already standing at the top, naked beneath the dressing gown he had pulled on.

'I thought I heard voices.'

'It–it's the police. They want to speak to both of us. Can you come down, Sam?' Her voice shook in spite of her resolve to stay calm.

'The police? What can they want at this time of night?' Then immediately, 'Is it Billy? Has he had an accident?'

'I–I don't know. Oh, Sam.' Her voice shook. 'Will you c–come down?' She sank onto the third stair up, knowing her legs wouldn't carry her any further right now. She clasped her head in her hands.

'I'll be with you in a second, sweetheart. Don't worry, Rosie. Billy is a good driver and we both know he's sensible or we'd never have bought him a car. I expect it's something minor.'

'Y–yes,' Rosemary whispered without conviction. No one was perfect. Billy was a teenager. How could they be sure he wouldn't test his wings like any fledgling?

While Sergeant Gregory and his colleague waited for Mrs Caraford to return to the room with her husband, he mentally reviewed the few facts they had gleaned so far. The car registration had provided the name of the owner of the car. The insurance confirmed the information was current and he was the only person insured to drive. That was not incontrovertible proof he was driving at the time of the accident though. That was something Sergeant Gregory would prefer to establish beyond doubt and it was not so simple when all three occupants had been thrown out of the car. Unfortunately there were few other clues relating to their identities. According to the report they had received from the scene of the accident, two of the young men in jeans and white polo shirts had no identification at all, no money, wallets or mobile phones. The third occupant had been wearing jeans and a grey sweatshirt with a hood and front pockets. The report was that he reeked of alcohol, but apart from a £2 coin, and a small sachet containing white powder in the pocket of his jeans, there was nothing to provide his identity.

The young constable at the scene had assumed the powder was some kind of drugs but Sergeant Gregory was too experienced to assume anything without proof. Forensics would tell them what they needed to know about substances, and the results of any blood tests which might have been taken.

'Our first priority is to be absolutely certain of the identities of these young men,' he said to Constable Jacobs, 'before we inform their families. The situation is too serious to risk jumping to conclusions.'

'Yes, sir,' Constable Jacobs agreed in a troubled voice. Sergeant Gregory had less than a year before he retired from the police force and at times like this he wished he was already finished, but he had no intention of making assumptions which could cause even more anguish to the families of the three young men. There would be plenty of that before the night was out, he thought grimly. He had always prided himself on being thorough, even if a few of his colleagues did consider him too strict.

He stood up as Sam and Rosemary Caraford entered the room together. The man had his arm around his wife's shoulders but his own face was tense and pale. The day had been hot and he looked exhausted after his day's labours.

'There has been a serious road accident involving the car which we now know is registered in your son's name,' he began and held up a hand when Sam would have questioned him. ' The car was heading north out of town but at this stage we are making enquiries to find out whether the vehicle could have been stolen, who was driving it and who the other two passengers were. Can you tell me where your son was going and whether he was likely to have any passengers?'

'He was collecting his friend, Liam Lennox, from Highfold Farm, and his sister, Fenella, but that was more than two hours ago. They were only going into town, to Gino's Coffee Bar, to celebrate passing their exams with their friends,' Sam said.

'A sister? One of them was a girl? How old would she be?'

'Fenella was sixteen last month,' Rosemary said.

'I see.' Sergeant Gregory frowned then looked across at Constable Jacobs. 'Contact the station, please. Better do it from the car.' He flicked a glance in the direction of the Carafords but Hazel Jacobs was sensitive enough to realize it was better if they didn't overhear, though it was looking more and more as though the Caraford boy was one of the three involved. 'Ask if they have any more details of the occupants and make sure there was not a girl with them.'

The couple who reported the accident had said the driver had been waving his arm out of the window while the car was travelling at speed on the wrong side of the road. It had swerved back to its own side and hit a tree full on, tearing away the front wing and side of the car. They thought that was when the first young man had been thrown out and killed. He was lying on that side of the road. The car had slewed back across the road and the couple thought it had rolled at least twice. One of the bodies had been several yards away. The one with the severed leg had been quite near the car, unconscious but still alive. Sergeant Gregory knew everyone at the scene would have concentrated on trying to save his life and get him to hospital, but he was fairly certain they would have made a thorough search for any other occupants. It was unlikely the body of a young girl would be overlooked unless she had been thrown some distance.

'If they were driving out of town they would be on

their way home,' Sam said, 'but you infer they were heading in the opposite direction?'

'As I said we are still making enquiries at this stage but your wife has confirmed the car is owned by your son, William Alexander Caraford, and we know it was being driven north on a straight stretch of the old motorway. The couple who phoned in to report the accident had taken the same route out of town but they had halted at the traffic lights so their car was some distance behind by the time it joined the same road heading north.' He didn't add that the Astra had driven through the lights at red and almost caused an accident with the oncoming traffic before it had even left the town.

'I see,' Sam said tightly. 'I can't think of any reason why Billy would be on that road.'

'Can you tell me what your son was wearing? Would he have any form of identification? A mobile phone perhaps?'

'He–he was wearing his jeans and a navy zip-up fleece. It has an inside zip pocket where he keeps his phone and his wallet. He always carried his school identity card and bus pass in his wallet. Liam had one almost identical. He was probably wearing his. They seem to be their favourite clothes at present.'

'Do they have hoods?'

'No.'

'Do you know what he was wearing under the jacket?'

'Yes, he was wearing his white polo shirt.' They all looked up as PC Hazel Jacobs returned to say there was no sign of a girl. She looked at the Carafords with compassion.

25

'The DVLA and our men at the scene are able to confirm from the photo licence that one of the young men at the scene is William Caraford, but they are unable to say whether he was driving.'

'Of course Billy would be driving. He's the only one insured to drive that car. He wouldn't risk letting anyone else drive it,' Sam said heatedly. 'Where is he? Is he hurt? We must see him.' Rosemary put a calming hand on his arm but her own face was chalky white now.

'Is he...? Has he...? Sam's right. We have to know. We need to see him. You must tell us what you know.'

'I understand how you both feel,' Sergeant Gregory said quietly. He looked up at his colleague and saw the distress in her eyes but she nodded her agreement. 'The truth is two of the young men are dead. The third is seriously injured in hospital and we have been unable to identify them. We are anxious not to make any mistakes with wrong identities and cause grief unintentionally.'

'I can understand that,' Sam said, his voice gritty with emotion, 'but this young woman has just confirmed that our son is involved. We have to know whether he is dead or alive. We need to see for ourselves,' he added desperately.

'You are both badly shaken,' Police Constable Jacobs said gently. 'We can take you to the hospital but you might prefer a member of your own family to drive you? Will you allow me to telephone your daughter, Rena?'

'You know Rena?' Rosemary asked, startled.

'I was at school with your twin daughters, Carol and Rena. May I telephone Rena and explain?'

'Y–yes please. Please do, but tell her to hurry.'

Both Rosemary and Sam knew they would never forget that night for as long as they lived. Billy was alive but severely injured and on the danger list. The doctors allowed them to see him but only briefly. They sensed even this concession was to confirm his identity and provide any medical details which might help them. They didn't want to leave his bedside but a kindly doctor drew them aside and explained it was vital to allow the nurses and doctors to proceed unhampered. His leg had been severed below the knee. While this had been serious in that it had resulted in considerable loss of blood, their main concern was his head injury. The doctor promised he would send for them if his condition changed. Meanwhile he strongly advised them to go home and rest.

'The doctor is right, Mum,' Rena said gently. She had driven them to the hospital. 'You both look exhausted and Dad will still want to make sure his animals aren't neglected.'

'That's true,' Rosemary agreed reluctantly. 'The cows will need to be brought in and milked. It's morning already. And you have your two little ones to look after and get ready for school, Rena.' She gave a huge sigh which ended in a choked little sob. 'Life has to go on for those of us who are left. If Billy is responsible for the death of his best friend....' She shuddered, unable to continue.

They were able to identify Liam and his stepbrother, Derek. Rosemary's heart ached with sorrow when she looked down on Liam's young face. None of them had been wearing seatbelts and his neck was broken. Derek had been scarcely recognizable. They couldn't understand why he had been with them, or why they had been travelling in the opposite direction to their homes. There were so many questions and no one able to answer them.

'I'll come back later,' Rena said as she dropped her parents back at Martinwold.

'You have your own responsibilities, Rena dear, with the garden centre to run and your children to get to school and nursery,' Rosemary said wearily. 'We're very grateful that you came with us.'

'I want to come back, Mum. I can't bear to think of our Billy with all those tubes attached and bandages round his head.' She shivered. 'I'll phone Australia and tell Carol what's happened. She'll want to know even though she is too far away to help. And Dad....' She hesitated. 'Do you mind if I phone Bengairney and tell Uncle Alex what has happened? I know things have been strained ever since you bought his share in Martinwold, but he thought the world of Billy, and he is your brother. You used to be so close. He will hear from other people.'

'Aye, you're right, lassie,' Sam sighed. 'Alex will be upset. Phone him later then.'

'I'll wait until breakfast time. Now you two must try and rest as the doctor advised.'

'I couldn't possibly rest,' Sam said when Rena had driven away. 'I have too many questions going round in my head, and too much grief in my heart to be able to sleep. The cows won't be ready to come in for milking for another hour or more but I think I'll bring them in anyway and get started. The milking has to be done and the hospital might send for us to go back. I need to keep busy.'

'Yes.' Rosemary looked up at him, her blue eyes dark with worry and fatigue. 'I'll come with you to round up the cows but first I'll switch on the kettle for a cup of coffee. Will you transfer the telephone through to my mobile so we don't miss any calls?'

'Good idea. I would appreciate your company, Rosie. I don't want to leave you alone, or to be alone myself.' Sam drew her close and buried his face against the soft warmth of her neck. They stood silently together for several minutes, each drawing comfort from the other.

'Sergeant Gregory and that nice young woman promised to let us know if they managed to find out any more details after they had broken the news to Jane and Syd Lennox.' She shuddered again. 'I don't know how I am going to face them.'

'I know, Rosie,' Sam said gruffly, his arms tightening around her. 'I can't believe Billy was responsible for such carnage, but if he was he–he'll wish he had d–died with them.'

'Don't! Don't say that, Sam, please.' Rosemary's voice broke as she looked up into his tired face. 'He and Liam were such good friends. They had so many plans for when they went to university. Only God knows what will happen now, but I just pray Billy will survive. I know it's selfish when the Lennoxes have lost both their sons.'

'I suppose it is and my heart aches for them,' Sam agreed, 'but while there's life there's hope and we both have to cling to that now, Rosie.'

'I know,' she whispered. 'Remember how thrilled we were to have a baby son after we had accepted there would be no more children?'

'Yes, it was like starting all over again. And he's dreamed about being a farmer since he could toddle.'

'He'll never be able to farm now, but I don't care. All I ask is that he will live,' Rosemary said, her voice breaking. Sam drew her close again and rocked her gently, giving and taking comfort from each other.

'I should never have quarrelled with Alex over buying out his share of this place. He had no wife or child so I thought he might sell to the highest bidder one day. We had Billy. I was ensuring his future, making sure Martinwold would be his. I should have trusted Alex.' He groaned. 'Now Billy might not even survive.'

The grass sparkled with dew as the sun began to creep over the horizon. The birds were coming to the end of their moulting season and beginning to sing their joyous songs again, but for once Sam and Rosemary were oblivious to the beauty of their surroundings. Most of the cows were still lying, contentedly chewing their cud. They showed no desire to rise and make their own way in for milking.

'I think they have a built-in time clock,' Rosemary said as she prodded yet another recumbent animal until she got onto her feet and stretched, before beginning a slow amble towards the field gate.

'They're not so stupid as people think,' Sam said. 'They know when their udders are full it's time to head towards the milking parlour. The milk yields will be down because we're more than an hour too early but I shall feel easier if I know they have been milked.'

'Yes, better for them to be an hour or so early

than several hours late if we get called back to the hospital.' Rosemary shivered, wondering what news would await them.

'We must be prepared to drop everything and go,' Sam said.

At quarter to six they turned out the last batch of cows from the milking parlour and Rosie crossed to the dairy to check the water troughs were filled ready to circulate around the parlour for cleaning. She saw the police car draw up to the house. She called to Sam and ran to meet them.

'Have you come from the hospital?' she asked breathlessly.

'We called in on our way here,' Sergeant Gregory said. 'The doctors say your son is holding his own but he is still unconscious.'

'Oh,' Rosemary said flatly and expelled a breath she hadn't realized she was holding. Her slim shoulders slumped.

'That is good news in the circumstances, Mrs Caraford,' Hazel Jacobs said gently.

'We called at Highfold Farm earlier, to speak to Mr and Mrs Lennox,' Sergeant Gregory said. 'They are deeply distressed.'

'They're bound to be,' Sam said gruffly as he joined them. 'Jane Lennox is a wonderful mother to all three of the children, and Syd thinks, er, thought the world of Derek.'

'So I gathered.' Sergeant Gregory frowned, choosing his words carefully. He couldn't tell them Mr Lennox was beyond reason. The man had refused to listen to anything they had to say. He insisted on blaming the Caraford boy. Nothing they could say would make him listen. Even worse was his fury when his daughter crept downstairs in her dressing gown hoping for news of Liam. It was evident she guessed something was wrong when she saw the police car from her bedroom window, but she had been totally unprepared for the news of her brother's death. The brutal way Mr Lennox told her had triggered a spontaneous reaction which convinced Sergeant Gregory she was telling the truth.

'No! No, oh no!' she had screamed. 'It's all Derek's fault. He stole the –' Mr Lennox had jumped to his feet as though he would strike her.

'The Lennox girl was safely at home,' Sergeant Gregory said now. 'Her friend's parents had given her a lift when her brother and your son didn't return to the coffee bar for her.'

'Thank God Fenella is safe,' Rosemary said fervently.

'Yes, she is safe, but she is very distressed.'

'I thought her father was going to strike her when she came downstairs to ask for news,' Constable Jacobs said quietly. 'He's a very disturbed man.'

'He didn't want her to talk to us, that's for sure,' Sergeant Gregory said grimly. 'We shall need to interview her again without him there, possibly on her own, or with her mother. We need to speak to her friend for confirmation too. Constable Jacobs escorted her back to bed and she was able to have a short conversation with her in her bedroom.' He looked at his colleague and gave a nod.

'Fenella said her elder brother came into the café and snatched the car key from your son. He ran out to the car and jumped into the driver's seat. Her own brother jumped into the passenger seat. She said they seemed to be arguing. She thought Liam was trying to persuade his brother to give back the car keys. Apparently your own son scrambled into the back as the car shot off down the High Street. She said the door swung open but he managed to grab it and slam it shut. She doesn't know what happened after that but she is convinced her step-brother would have been driving the car at the time of the accident. Mr Lennox adamantly refuses to accept her version of what happened.' Constable Jacobs said anxiously. 'She was dreadfully upset.'

'We need to get more statements, and hopefully some corroboration, but my guess is Mr Lennox is unwilling to accept any version except his own, even though he was not there,' Sergeant Gregory said grimly.

'All this may not be much comfort when your son is so badly injured,' Constable Jacobs said gently, 'but we're going off duty now. We thought you should know we don't think your son was driving at the time of the accident.'

'Whatever happens to Billy, it is a great relief to hear that. He would never have forgiven himself if he was responsible for Liam's death,' Sam said.

'Thank you both for taking time to come and tell us,' Rosemary said gratefully. She looked up at Constable Jacobs. She turned her troubled blue eyes to Sergeant Gregory. 'Would you...? Can I make you some breakfast, or a hot drink?'

'No, thank you, Mrs Caraford, but it is a kind offer when you have so much on your mind,' Sergeant Gregory said with a gentleness his colleagues would never have believed. 'It has been a stressful night all round. We're both ready to finish our shift and get home to bed.'

THREE

Rosemary and Sam took turns at spending as much time at Billy's bedside as the doctors would allow, with relief from Rena when she could get away from her own responsibilities, but it was several days before they were allowed to break the news of Liam's death and even then Billy was still so groggy from his injuries and the heavy doses of medication they were unsure whether he understood. For the first time in Sam's life the farm and the animals were a secondary consideration. The harvest had continued with the cooperation of the local contractor and his men. He and Rosemary had milked the cows each morning before going to the hospital.

'Our own men are subdued too,' he said as he and Rosemary sought comfort in each other's arms a week later. 'They're wondering how Billy will accept the loss of his leg and the end of his dream to take over the farm. It's a bitter blow to all of us but at least he is alive, thank God. The doctors seem fairly certain the blow to his head has not done permanent damage.'

'We have a lot to be thankful for,' Rosemary said,

determined to look on the bright side, even though her heart ached for Billy and his youthful dreams, and for Jane Lennox, Liam's mother. 'Billy's careers advisor telephoned from school to enquire after him. He says Billy will be able to resume his education at university next year and he will do everything he can to help him choose an alternative career. He has offered to visit him in hospital when Billy feels up to it. In the short term I think the news of Liam's death will affect him as badly as losing his leg.'

'Yes. He's beginning to think more clearly now they are reducing the medication, but he does have a lot of injuries, sweetheart. At least the drugs have given them a chance to heal. He was lucky the broken ribs didn't pierce his lung as the doctors first feared.'

'He is lucky to be alive at all,' Rosemary said, shuddering. 'One of the younger doctors said it helped the patient's spirits if they could regain some sort of mobility as soon as possible after an amputation but the broken ribs and having his arm in plaster will delay any attempts at crutches. I'm not sure Billy fully realizes that he has lost his leg yet though.'

'Time,' Sam sighed, 'that's what we're all going to need, time and patience. Jo Finkle has proved himself a friend in need yet again.'

'Yes, he may be an old man but his eyes are as sharp as ever,' Rosemary said.

'My father always said he could rely on him through thick and thin.'

Although in his eighties, Johan Finkle still walked up to Martinwold from his cottage every day to help with any odd jobs he could still manage to do. As soon as he heard about Billy's accident he had taken it upon himself to count and check the young animals in the fields each day, relieving Sam of that responsibility. He had begun working for Sam's parents when he was a young prisoner of war. He had known Sam and Alex, and their sister Tania, since they were born. They were all the family he had. He had offered his prayers when Rosemary was desperately ill before the twins were born, and he had rejoiced when Billy had arrived in the world eleven years later. Now he was as distressed by Billy's accident as Billy's own parents.

It didn't seem possible that more anguish was yet to come. Rosemary had known Jane Lennox since Liam was at nursery school and she knew Jane would be stricken with grief over his death. She couldn't believe Mr Lennox had forbidden her to visit, or even speak to her on the telephone, but Jane managed to phone from her mobile while she was out in the garden early one morning.

'Fenella is dreadfully upset,' Jane said, her voice shaking as she struggled to control her own emotions. 'She knows Derek was to blame but Syd is so bitter he is blaming anyone and everyone except Derek. I–I'm afraid he has convinced himself it was Billy's fault.'

'Surely not!' Rosemary gasped. 'How can he think that?'

'I'm dreadfully sorry, Rosemary. You and Sam have always been such good neighbours but Sydney is blaming you for buying Billy a car of his own. He – he's being completely unreasonable. He refuses to speak to Fenella. He says she must tell the police Derek was not to blame. She w–wanted to visit Billy in hospital but he is threatening to put both of us out of the house if we speak to any of you.'

'Surely Syd must realize Fenella had to tell the truth to the police. She and Liam were so close. She must be full of grief, even without having to face questions and an enquiry,' Rosemary said. 'I heard her friend Amanda gave the same account to the police so Fenella couldn't have lied, even if she had wanted to. Surely Syd must understand that?'

'There's no reasoning with him. I–I'm afraid of him, Rosemary. He – he's going to need some kind of help to get over this. He refuses to speak to Doctor Jamieson, let alone accept any medication.'

'I'm so sorry, Jane. I wish I knew what to do to help. Syd's attitude must be making your own heartbreak over Liam even harder to bear.'

'Yes, it is, but I wanted you to understand why I can't keep in touch. Try to understand, Rosemary dear, it is not what I want, or what Fenella wants, but we're doing our best not to aggravate him while he is in such a difficult frame of mind.'

After Jane's phone call, Rosemary knew she should have been prepared but instead she burst into tears when the Reverend McCally called at Martinwold and gravely asked her and Sam not to attend the funerals of Derek and Liam Lennox.

'I'm so sorry,' he apologized for the fifth time. 'Syd Lennox is not thinking straight in his grief. It is at his request that I am here.' It had not been a request. It had been a command, accompanied by more blaspheming than the elderly minister had heard for many a year, a command instructing him to come to Martinwold and tell the Carafords they were not welcome at the funerals of his sons and if they appeared at the church the funeral would be cancelled and he would tell the world their son was to blame for the deaths of his two sons. In his own bitter way he was doing that already.

Rumours were rife in the parish and surrounding villages but the Revd McCally had heard a first-hand account from Mrs Pearson, the mother of Fenella's friend, Amanda. The two girls had seen Derek snatch the key and drive off at a crazy speed. The elderly minister feared Mr Lennox was on the verge of a mental breakdown, even allowing for his grief at the death of his own son, Derek, and the son he had adopted and given his name. Jane was a good woman who had done her best to fulfil her promises and care for him and his child. She didn't deserve the misery she was suffering now over the death of her own beloved Liam and it was intensified by her husband banning her from seeing or speaking to her friends and neighbours.

It was an even worse shock when Sam and Rosemary saw the photograph of the crashed car in one of the newspapers and read the account. It reported that drink and drugs were involved but Rosemary stared in horror at the inference that Billy, the only survivor, was the one to blame.

'Whoever the reporter is he has been careful not to state categorically that Billy is to blame,' Sam said bitterly, 'but he has made it as sensational as he can and he doesn't care about the hurt he is causing, or what this might do to Billy if he reads it.'

'We must hope no one mentions it to him,' Rosemary said. 'I doubt if he sees newspapers while he is in a room on his own. I believe the story must have come from Syd Lennox.'

It was inevitable that Liam's death would have a grave effect on Billy once he was able to take it in. They had been close friends since they started nursery and then primary school. One afternoon he was lying half sleeping, half dreaming as he gazed through the window into the distance. Beyond the hospital grounds he glimpsed the river, winding its way past the trees and the green grass in the park. He and Liam had enjoyed being in the rowing club. He wondered if he would be able to row without his leg. They didn't have to be competitors. They could do it for fun, just the two of them. Surely he would still be able to swim? Anyway, Liam would help him get in and out of the boat. Good old Liam.... His brain cleared. Reality hit him with cold, hard facts that he had subconsciously thrust away. Liam was dead. He would never see him again. They would never do anything together, never share a joke, never laugh together, never help each other with their schoolwork. Never.

'Oh God!' he groaned aloud. 'No,' he whispered hoarsely, 'no, not Liam....' But there was no escaping the truth, which had been buried and blurred by the drugs. He wanted to howl like a baby. He turned his head away to hide the hot stinging tears which flooded his eyes. He wanted to turn on his side, away from the blasted corridor window where everybody could, and did, look in as though he was a goldfish in a bowl. The pain in his chest hurt as he tried to turn and he rubbed his eyes angrily and kept his good arm over his face so that no one would see his unmanly tears. He felt there was a weight in his breast, hard and painful as though all his grief and loss had crystalized into indestructible rock.

His mother noticed the change in him as soon as she visited but she was too sensitive to probe.

'He seems so quiet and withdrawn into himself,' she reported anxiously to Sam when she arrived back home from visiting. 'It's as though a veil has descended. As though he has left his youth behind overnight.'

'Well, his life has been turned upside-down. His plans – everything has changed,' Sam said, drawing her into his arms to comfort her. 'The doctors told him yesterday they need to remove a bit more of his leg because it's not healing properly. He seemed to accept it philosophically, or so I believed, but it's a sobering thought for anybody, let alone an active young man. Losing a leg, changing your life and youthful dreams, above all losing his best friend, they're enough to make anybody withdrawn. All we can do is let him know we love him and we're thankful he is alive.'

'I suppose so, but my heart aches for him,' Rosemary said, 'and I feel so helpless. I can't take him in my arms and kiss him better like I did when he was a baby.'

'He is bound to miss Liam's company. They were such good friends.'

'Jane phoned earlier today. Syd was out. He had gone to the bank so she took the chance to telephone. She says Fenella and her friend would like to visit Billy in hospital but they'll need to go in on the bus as it would make things worse if she drove them there and Syd found out.'

'Jane is in a difficult situation but some young company might help Billy,' Sam mused. 'He might be able to talk to Fenella and her friend about the accident. I think he needs to get it out in the open, like poison. They were the only ones who actually saw what happened.'

'That's true, but Sergeant Gregory took his statement and he said it tallied with the account the girls had given. Thank goodness Billy has never read any of the newspaper reports. The local paper was not quite as bad. At least it hasn't passed judgement until there has been an enquiry.'

Rosemary would have been dismayed to know Billy had read the newspaper reports. One of the young nurses had been furious at the injustice of it. She knew Billy had not had drink or drugs in him when he arrived at the hospital. She wanted to write to the paper on his behalf but both Billy and the senior nurse had asked her to ignore the reports.

'It only prolongs the story,' Billy said with a note of bitterness. 'My parents are worried enough without reading all that speculation.'

'We shall be removing the cast from your broken arm in a day or two,' the senior nurse told him, sensing that he needed a boost. It was a small enough encouragement, considering he would have a long way to go before he was able to get around unaided with a prosthetic leg. She knew there were times when he had a struggle to hide his dejection and she admired him for that. He had proved a good patient. Even in the early stages he had only complained if the pain became unbearable. Breathing had become less painful as his fractured ribs healed. He was beginning to consider the future.

'There's you trying to protect the parents, and there's Mum and Dad thinking they have prevented you from reading any of the newspaper reports,' Rena said wryly one day when she visited alone. 'So, now you're feeling a bit more like the brother I know and love, would you mind if I bring Fenella and her friend to see you? Her father has forbidden her to come but I could pick them up at the Academy on my way here. They get a half-day study leave now they are in fifth year. According to the rare conversations between Jane and Mum, Fenella has been desperate to visit ever since the accident but her dad has forbidden any contact with our family. I suspect Fenella is afraid you'll think she was responsible for the newspaper reports.'

'I'd never think that. It was all Derek's stupid fault. Fenella tried to warn us as soon as she saw him. Liam said he had been trying to make trouble all day. He was probably jealous because Liam and Fenella had both done so well in their exams,' he added bitterly, 'but he acted like a madman.' It was the first time he had managed to mention Liam's name without feeling his throat choking with emotion. 'We were getting up ready to leave. Derek snatched the car key. I can't talk to Mum and Dad about it but I can tell you, sis. I've never felt so frightened in my life. I've wished and wished Liam and I had let him take the car and kill himself if that's what he wanted. He went crazy. The more Liam protested the wilder he drove, waving his arm out of the window and hallooing at the clouds. We were flung about the car like rag dolls. I grabbed my seatbelt but I didn't have time to find the slot, let alone fasten it. I was flung one way and then back again as he turned right out of the town. I was thrown across the back seat and I braced my leg against the back of Liam's seat. Suddenly we were heading straight at a tree. God, Rena....' He buried his face in his hands for a moment. 'As long as I live I shall never forget that last glimpse of Liam's face. It was petrified with fear, and Derek was cackling like an idiot.'

'He was an idiot. Drink or drugs seem to make idiots of the best of people,' Rena said quietly, 'but I'm glad you've been able to talk to me about it, Billy. So you think it's all right for Fenella to visit? You don't mind?'

'No, I'd like to see her and Amanda and hear what they're saying about it. Mum and Dad avoid mentioning the Lennoxes but Rev. McCally came in for a visit and he let a few things slip. Did you know he had to visit Mum and Dad and ask them to stay away from Liam's funeral?' His voice broke. 'That's not what Liam would have wanted. He always said Martinwold was his second home and my parents always made him welcome.'

'It's impossible to keep secrets in a small community.' Rena sighed. 'If you ask me it's better to be open about things. Mr Lennox seems to be blaming our family for everything. It's my guess he is at least partly responsible for the horrible insinuations in the newspapers. Mum says his grief is driving him crazy.'

'I see.' Billy frowned then met Rena's eyes steadily. 'I think he was getting a bit that way even before the crash. Derek had been going off the rails ever since he was in second year at the Academy, but Liam said he had been worse this past year. His father must have known he was drinking, even if he didn't realize he was taking drugs, but he refused to hear any criticism. He – he hit Liam when he dared to criticize.'

'Poor Liam,' Rena said with a catch in her voice. 'One of your teachers has been to see Mum and Dad, you know. He said Liam had a brilliant brain and he knew exactly what he wanted to do with his life. I'd better warn you he also thinks you would be wasting your time doing agriculture now. He told them you have the ability to do almost anything with science with three A-grade science subjects and A passes in three other subjects. Mum and Dad seem to agree that you should apply for a different course too. Accountancy they're thinking, so that you can sit down to do your work.'

'No way!' Billy stared at her. 'Dad knows all I've ever wanted to do is farm. I've been thinking I should skip university altogether.' Rena looked uncomfortable.

'Dad doesn't think you'll be able to farm with – with only one leg,' she said gently.

'Well, I know some things won't be so easy, and maybe some will be impossible. I'm not so stupid that I think it will not make any difference, but farming is all I've dreamed about for as long as I can remember. When I used to stay at Bengairney for my holidays, Grandpa Caraford used to say I would make a first-rate stockman one day. He said I had good observational skills and they were as important as doing the hard graft. I didn't really understand what he meant then. I shall have to find ways around the things I can't manage myself and ways to compensate.'

'I'm only warning you to be prepared for some opposition,' Rena said. 'It has been a big blow to Dad too.

His plans have centred around you and the future of Martinwold, almost since you were born, certainly since you showed such an interest in the farm and the animals. That was the reason he and Uncle Alex quarrelled, as you know. He insisted on buying Uncle Alex's share of Martinwold, and each of them farming separately, to make sure it would belong to you one day.'

'I forgot to tell you Uncle Alex came in to visit me again this week. That's the second time he's been, but I was only vaguely aware of him the first time. I didn't know whether I should mention it to Mum and Dad.'

'I'm sure it would be all right to tell them now. The accident has been a terrible shock to everyone. This sort of thing brings people to their senses and puts things in perspective. It was a shame they quarrelled. Uncle Alex was such fun when Carol and I went to stay at Bengairney when Granny and Grandpa were alive. He always said he would never marry. He used to tease Mum and say she was the only girl he'd ever wanted to marry. It annoyed Dad a bit. I think there was some truth in it now that I'm grown up and married myself. I suspect Uncle Alex was hurt that Dad didn't trust him to pass his share of Martinwold to you, without them needing to make it all official and exchange money and deeds and everything.'

'Well, I wish he and Dad hadn't quarrelled. I enjoyed his visit. He discussed the farm and his herd and he's the only one who still assumes I shall follow my dreams. Anyway, what did Mum say about my future?' Billy asked drily.

'She's thankful that you're alive and that the head

injuries were not as serious as the doctors feared. So long as you're able to do something which satisfies you, I don't think Mum will interfere.'

'Well, the only thing which will satisfy me is farming,' Billy said stubbornly. 'Thanks for preparing me for some opposition from Dad, Rena.'

Fenella Lennox was nervous when she entered the small hospital ward alone. Amanda was off school with a summer cold so Rena had dropped Fenella off at the hospital while she did her shopping in the town.

'Hello, Fenella.' Billy felt wary, even though he had known her all her life and had always liked Liam's young sister. He was unsure what her reaction might be. Did she share her father's opinion that he was to blame for Liam's death because he had his own car that night?

'Oh Billy, I've been desperate to see you and beg your forgiveness.'

'My forgiveness, Fen?' He was surprised. Her eyes widened at his use of her shortened name. 'Sorry,' he said. 'Liam always called you Fen when he was talking about you.'

'I–I don't mind. It was his – his pet name for me. I miss him so much, Billy.' Before either of them realized it, they were weeping together.

'Me too. Oh God, you don't know how much I wish we'd never jumped in the car after Derek. Liam only did it for me, I know he did.'

'What's all this then?' a voice interrupted. 'Are you upsetting my patient, young lady?' Nurse Palmer asked, but cheerfully. 'You're supposed to cheer him up, you know.'

'I–I know. I–I'm sorry. I didn't mean to get upset.' Both Billy and Fenella reached for a tissue and blew their noses and wiped away tears.

'This is my friend's young sister, Fenella Lennox,' Billy said. 'I d–don't know what came over me. I haven't done that with anybody else.' Except an occasional night when you thought no one knew, Nurse Palmer thought.

'It will do you a world of good, young man. You have been too buttoned up. Far too controlled for a young man who has come through such a trauma. Tears help to wash away the grief, you know. There's no need to be ashamed of them. It's natural to miss a well-loved brother or a good friend. Take as long as you like, young lady. I'll come back later with my charts.' She walked briskly away, leaving Fenella and Billy staring awkwardly at each other until Billy summoned a wobbly smile.

'I thought you might blame me after the stuff I read in the papers.'

'Oh Billy, I hoped you'd never see the papers. I–I think my father was to blame for a lot of that. He's been terrible. He's making Mum's life hell, in fact. Mine too, when I'm at home, but at least I get away to school. Mum sent you some sweets and some grapes, by the way. She would have come to see you too only it would cause more trouble. I hate him when he's like this. He must realize it was all Derek's fault.'

'Derek is dead,' Billy said flatly. 'He can't speak for himself, even if he had wanted to. Mr Lennox knows that. I expect he's clinging to the image of Derek he has in his memory.' He couldn't help the bitterness when he thought of the contrast with Liam, so innocent, so honest and truthful.

'Well, I'm working terribly hard at school. If I can get enough higher grades to go to university after fifth year I shall go a year early and escape from the awful atmosphere.'

'But you're not seventeen until next summer.'

'I know, but Glasgow might accept me if my grades are all As. The sooner I can get away from home the better. It's a long course anyway to be a vet so a year early would help. I don't know how Mum can stick things at home. She knows how I feel. She hopes my father will get better with time but she does understand how I miss Liam and how angry I feel because my father thinks he's the only one who is suffering. Mum says if things are still as bad by next summer she might help me buy a flat. I could rent out a room to help with expenses and she might come to stay sometimes for the weekend. I'd like that. There's nothing to keep me here now,' she added bitterly.

'I'm sure you're clever enough, Fen, if you're sure it's what you want,' Billy said, 'but you always said you wanted to go to Edinburgh.'

'I know but that was mainly because you and Liam would have been there.' She summoned a smile. 'I thought I'd get lifts home. Now all I want is to get away.'

'I hate to see you so miserable, Fenella.'

'I miss Liam terribly.' She caught her breath on a sob and Billy reached out and stroked her hand.

'I shall have to wait until next year too if I still decide to go for a degree. Part of me thinks I shouldn't bother then I could go home and get on with my life.'

'Oh, surely you'll have even more need to get a

degree now, Billy? Mr Fisher said I was to tell you he'd like to come in and talk to you about a change of career. He says you have lots of options with your exam results.'

'He always did consider agriculture was a waste of time,' Billy said drily.

'Only for you, because you've done so well at school.'

'Well, farming is all I've ever wanted to do, whatever anybody says,' Billy stated belligerently. Fenella reached forward and squeezed his hand.

'I know that, Billy, but even your parents don't think it will be possible now – now....'

'Now that I shall have a peg leg, you mean,' Billy finished bitterly. 'Don't be afraid to mention it, Fen. I'm learning to accept it but it doesn't mean to say I shall let it change my whole life. Think of all the servicemen who lose limbs and still lead useful lives. Think of all those children in Africa who have stepped on mines and lost both their legs. At least I can still see and think and I have two good arms.' He grimaced wryly. 'As Rev. McCally says, I have to count my blessings.'

'I know. I don't think it will be easy, though, carrying buckets of milk from the parlour or feeding calves when all they seem to want is to knock you over and spill the milk getting at the bucket. And what about calving cows when there's problems?'

'If you make a good vet, maybe I'll send for you to do that.' For the first time since the accident some of the strain and tension left Billy's lean face and a glimmer of a smile hovered around his mouth. Passing the ward, Sister Palmer nodded with satisfaction. That child in her school uniform seemed to be helping her patient after all.

'Do you mind if I come again and bring Amanda with me, Billy? So long as my father doesn't find out, of course, and if Rena will give us a lift again? Some of the boys talked about coming too. Jim Finlay and Phil Maxwell are staying on at school to try for better grades.'

'I'm not going to be here much longer. I'd have been mobile quicker if I hadn't broken my arm and a couple of ribs. I'm hoping to get home as soon as I can manage the crutches.' He hated having to depend on the nurses every time he wanted the toilet, or anything else. He was impatient to try anything which would give him a measure of independence.

'Well, you played enough rugby so I suppose you should have strong shoulders to take your weight,' Fenella said.

'Rugby.' He groaned. 'There'll be no more of that, or football. Oh, God.' He bowed his head in his hands in a gesture of despair. 'Sometimes I wish....'

'No! Don't say it, Billy. Never, ever wish you'd died like Liam.' Fenella's voice caught in her throat. 'There's so many other things you can do. You have to think positively or you'll be as bad as my father,' she added. 'Every word he utters is something negative. You'll still be able to sing when you come to parties. You still have your brains. Promise me you'll make the most of what you have, Billy. It is what Liam would have wanted. You know it is.'

'I suppose so,' Billy muttered. He pulled himself up straighter in the bed. 'All right then, Miss Lennox, I shall start by doing exercises to get the strength back in my arms and shoulders and I shall tell that pretty little physio I intend to get moving under my own steam as soon as the doctors say my ribs have healed properly.'

'You're sounding more cheerful, Billy,' Rena said, coming in to join them. 'I believe your visit has done him good, Fenella. Let me know if you want a lift another day. It's no problem. I drive past your school on my way from Langton Gardens anyway when I'm heading for Dumfries.'

FOUR

The months which followed were a period of ups and many downs for Billy as he struggled to regain some independence. He was dismayed to find his own parents seriously believed he would change all his plans and ambitions and pursue a sedentary career. His mother suggested law or accountancy and he almost wished he had not worked so hard at school and done so well in his exams. Even more discouraging was his father pointing out the tasks he would never be able to do around the farm, such as chasing the cattle when they were moved from field to field or loaded in a lorry to be sold: calving cows could be stubborn to manage, especially when they were in difficulties and suffering pain, and even doing the artificial insemination could be risky if one caught him off balance.

'Then I shall have to go back to using the artificial insemination service,' he said stubbornly. 'There has to be a way round the things I can't do myself. If that pilot, Bader, could fly an aeroplane without any legs then surely I deserve to have a go at following my dream to farm when I've only lost half a leg. I shall have to be a good manager and make sure I employ men who can do the tasks I can't do myself,' he argued. 'Uncle Alex believes I can do it. He says a good manager is worth three men.'

'We don't employ any spare labour on farms these days for you to manage. In fact fewer men want work on dairy farms with early mornings and seven days a week,' Sam said. 'Fate usually guarantees it is when a man is off that you need him most. I'm lucky. Your mother has always been there, and willing, when I needed an extra pair of hands, as your grandmother was for your grandfather at Bengairney.'

'I suppose you think I'm not likely to get a wife at all if I'm a peg-leg farmer,' Billy snapped. He thought about Fenella Lennox. She had promised to visit him again in hospital but she hadn't come back. Neither had she visited him since he had come home. Of course, she was only a schoolgirl but deep down he was hurt by Fenella's absence because she was one of the few people who really understood what had happened that fateful night. More than that, she knew how much he missed Liam. He had thought they could share their loss. He shrugged. He would stand on his own feet. He gave a mental grimace. He didn't have feet any more, only a foot.

'Of course, I didn't mean you wouldn't get a wife,' his father denied hastily. 'At least not on account of your leg. I meant most modern women prefer a career away from the farm these days. We all have to face facts, Billy. It's breaking your mother's heart to see you so frustrated. All our plans and dreams were for you to take over the farm from us and carry on. Now we count our blessings and we're thankful you're alive.'

In his heart Billy knew his parents only wanted what they thought was best for him. After all, the continuing future of Martinwold had been his father's dream, as well as his own, and they'd had plans to continue breeding and improving the Martinwold herd.

Uncle Alex, Aunt Tania and his father had grown up at Bengairney and his mother had spent all her spare time there too. She had always said what a happy home it was when they were young. It was a rented farm but Uncle Alex had continued to live there with his parents until they died. He didn't have a wife to help him, but he had built up one of the best herds in Scotland, especially since he had farmed alone. Billy knew his own parents had moved into Martinwold when they married but the two farms had been run together as one business until the rift between his father and uncle.

Billy knew his father had borrowed enough money from the bank to buy Uncle Alex's share of Martinwold and the two farms had been run independently since then. Having been bought out, Uncle Alex had ample capital to make improvements at Bengairney if he wanted.

'I haven't made any changes,' he explained to Billy during one of their discussions at the hospital. 'I know your father thought I would but I have no wife or family, except for you, laddie, and Bengairney is a rented farm. Improvements would increase the value of the farm and if it ever comes to sell I'd like to be the one to buy it. There will be time enough for changes if that happens. Meanwhile I reckon land is about the best investment a man can make, especially if he's a farmer.' Their discussion had helped Billy understand the rift but he was sorry he had been the unwitting cause.

On another visit his uncle had admitted the money from selling his share of Martinwold had come in useful in some respects.

'I spent a good bit of money buying in new bloodlines for the Bengairney herd but I'm reaping the rewards now. They are proving a great success. In fact if I sold my herd now I could afford to retire, but I enjoy the challenge too much to give up farming yet.'

'You couldn't possibly give up, Uncle Alex,' Billy said. 'You're too young and you'd be miserable without your cows.'

'Aye, I suppose I would, though I don't think that when I've to get up in the middle of the night to calve a heifer when its blowing a blizzard.' They grinned at each other, knowing everything had its ups and downs. Alex Caraford was well known in markets all over the country and his animals continually brought in the highest prices. Two of the Bengairney bulls had been approved for artificial insemination and they had brought in yet more income from semen sales.

Billy knew his father's hopes and dreams had been concentrated on himself. As an only son he would carry on the Caraford name and together they had planned to make a success of both Martinwold farm and the Martinwold herd. So why could his parents not accept that he still wanted to farm, even if he was a cripple?

*

During his enforced year at home, Billy tried too hard to prove that he was normal and could do everything a more able-bodied man could do. Twice he had ignored the signs, and the pain, and walked too long and consequently inflamed the stump where his artificial leg fitted. The doctor at the hospital had warned him that if he continued to ignore their advice this could have serious consequences. If the stump did not heal and harden sufficiently, he might need to remove more of his leg, including his knee joint.

At times like this Billy sought the privacy of his bedroom. He felt like bursting into tears and once or twice his spirits had been so low he thought he would have been better off like Liam. His collie Bib seemed to sense his young master's need for comfort and invariably crept upstairs to scratch softly on the bedroom door. Billy always welcomed the dog's undemanding affection. 'Sometimes I think you're the only one who is pleased to have me home, Bib,' he often said, stroking his silky ears. When they were young he and his sisters had never been allowed to have pets in their bedrooms. His mother had insisted animals were happiest in their own beds and if the children wanted to share them they could go to the kennel, or the rabbit hutch, or the cage. Now Bib went upstairs in search of her master and no one commented. He didn't know his mother's heart ached for him, or that she understood how much he needed the silent sympathy of his dog. Billy had named him Bib because he had a white patch beneath his chin with a narrow white strip on either side which Billy fancied looked like a bib with strings attached. Apart from a tan patch over one ear and eye, the rest of Bib was a glossy black. Bib's mother had been an excellent dog for working with cattle but Sam was her master. She had never worked for anyone else and she was getting too old for much work now so Bib would have been a welcome addition to Martinwold, if only he was more biddable. Unfortunately he was too enthusiastic when it came to rounding up the cattle and they did not need, or appreciate, an eager young dog continuously circling and snapping at their heels. A well-trained cow dog could save a lot of time, and in Billy's case a lot of effort, but frequently he had had to leave his canine friend tied in his kennel while he walked the extra distance to rouse a few contented cows who sleepily ignored the rest making their way in for milking.

'Maybe we'll get a quad bike when you come home from university – that is if you still want to farm,' his father had said, 'but we'll wait and see.'

Alex had started visiting Martinwold again since Billy had been home.

'Take every opportunity they offer while you're at university, Billy,' he advised one Sunday afternoon when they were alone in the sitting room after lunch. 'If they arrange farm visits or trips abroad, grasp the chance to see how other farmers do things. There's always something new to learn for all of us. You never know what ideas you might pick up. And the same with any extra study modules, which might be useful. It doesn't matter whether you take an exam in them or not but knowledge is never wasted. Of course I wouldn't like to see you cramming so much in you have no time to enjoy yourself, laddie,' he added with a grin. 'But you must make sure your studies come first to get a good degree.' He began to laugh. 'Lecture over. I confess this is a case of do as I say, not as I did. I couldn't wait to get on with my life and all I wanted was to get home and farm.'

'But you have no regrets?'

'No – at least not about studying, or being a farmer.'

At the end of April Alex Caraford telephoned Martinwold to pass on some unexpected news.

'The young laird has died,' he said without preamble.

'The young laird! He's dead?' Sam echoed. 'But when? I mean, I'd heard he was unwell and that he and his sister were staying at Scarth Manor again, but I didn't know it was that serious.'

'No, I don't think anyone realized he was terminally ill,' Alex said in troubled tones, 'but the housekeeper up at the Manor has spread the word, and my Mrs Walters couldn't wait to tell me when she arrived for work at Bengairney this morning.' Mrs Walters, an honest and efficient woman who did plain cooking for Alex five mornings a week, was friends with Mrs Brex, housekeeper up at the Manor.

'It doesn't seem many years since the old laird died,' Sam mused. 'Father insisted all three of us should go to the funeral and pay our respects because we had been tenants at Bengairney for so long.'

'Aye. There were more tenants then. They were all there.'

'Rosemary used to know the laird and his sister when they were all younger. They were twins. I'm sure she will want to go to the funeral. Shall we pick you up and we can all go together, if you let us know when the funeral will be?'

'Thanks, Sam.' There was relief in Alex's voice. 'I didn't fancy going on my own. There's so few other tenants left.'

'I know. They sold some of the farms to pay the inheritance tax when the old laird died.'

'Home Farm is the biggest, and the best, and they still have it in their own hands. They employ a manager,' Alex said. 'Apart from that they only own Bengairney and Highfold, and the smallholding at West Charmwood.'

'Trevor and Ellen Wilshaw are a few years younger than Rosemary, and you, Alex,' Sam said, 'so they can't be fifty yet either. It's too young to die.'

'Nobody has any say in these things,' Alex said flatly. 'Youth will not stop them having more taxes to pay, unless the old laird made some sort of provision.'

'I doubt if he would do that, otherwise he would have prepared for settling his own affairs. He had plenty of years to think about it. Are you thinking they might sell Bengairney this time?'

'It's a possibility, don't you think?'

'It sure is. As a sitting tenant you'd get a bargain, Alex. You would buy it, wouldn't you? I mean, it's too good a chance to miss.'

'Well, land is a good investment but I've neither wife nor child to consider, or to pass it on to.'

'Maybe not, but when you get tired of farming you'd get a good profit with vacant possession. You used to fancy seeing something of the world. You could take a world cruise.'

'I suppose so.' Alex hesitated, then hurried into

speech. 'I was a silly bugger for resenting you wanting to buy my share of Martinwold. I can see that now. I thought you had the wife I'd always wanted, and then you got a son. Then you wanted to own the land we'd all worked so bloody hard to buy when Mr Turner died. I suppose I was jealous, but I was too angry to see that at the time.' Sam was silent for several seconds.

'That makes two silly buggers, then – you and me both. I was afraid you'd get married and have children of your own. I wanted to control things to make sure Billy inherited Martinwold.'

'But that was the thing, Sam. I knew I'd never marry. I thought you should have trusted me to pass on my share of Martinwold to Billy.'

'Never say never, Alex. Twelve years ago you were only in your early thirties and still dancing like you did when you were eighteen, with half the females eager to partner you. We were sure you'd get married and have children of your own.'

'Instead I'm a confirmed, crusty old bachelor,' Alex said.

'I'm not so sure about that. I'll bet Ginny Green would give up her veterinary practice and marry you tomorrow if you asked her. She always had a crush on you, even when she was a schoolgirl.'

'Ah, Sam, you'd organize the world if you could,' Alex said, but he chuckled and Sam was pleased to hear that. 'Ginny is a grand lassie and a good vet, but I don't love her and it's too late now.'

'It's never too late,' Sam said, 'but I've learned my lesson.' His hand trembled as he held the phone. 'As soon as Billy started school I was making plans. Then we nearly lost him. I never want to live through a nightmare like that again. I tell you, Alex, I thank God every day that he's alive, and it doesn't matter anymore whether he wants to farm or not so long as he's here and happy.'

'I know. It seems to me he's still as keen to farm though. I reckon you'll have to support him, whatever problems he has to face.'

'Aye, we're learning to accept that. But back to Bengairney – you would buy if it is to sell, wouldn't you, Alex? I mean you'll have at least half the capital from your share of Martinwold, and if I can help at all you know I will.'

'Thanks, but the money wouldn't be a problem,' Alex said. 'We'll have to wait and see. The laird and his sister have a business of their own as land agents and auctioneers in Gloucestershire but I doubt if they'll have had time to accumulate enough spare wealth to settle taxes in the time since the old laird died. Their income from the estate would be drastically reduced with so few farms. Bengairney has been well maintained, I'll grant the laird that. All the buildings are in good repair. Mrs Walters keeps hinting that the house is needing modernized, of course. I believe the Lennoxes' place at Highfold has been well maintained too. The Manor House is the one most in need of repairs, from what I hear, even though it's their own home.'

'They weren't living there,' Sam said. 'I suppose that makes a difference. Sir Trevor wasn't married, was he?'

'Not that we ever heard,' Alex said, 'but Mrs Walters reckons there's a child, about eleven or twelve. Apparently she's staying with friends in Gloucester until the end of the school term. I don't know which of the Wilshaw twins she belongs to, though. I'm surprised the gossipy Mrs Brex doesn't know. They had a private nurse in to help care for Sir Trevor towards the end and it sounds as though Mrs Brex's nose was put out of joint having to cook for her.'

'Some folks don't know when they're well off. She'll have had things too easy when none of the family were living at the Manor.'

It was the longest conversation Sam and Alex had had in recent years and Rosemary could tell Sam was pleased, as she was too, but she was genuinely sorry to hear about the death of Trevor Wilshaw. It was a long time since she had seen either him or his sister but she still remembered the mischievous twinkle in their eyes when they had come to lunch as her mother's guests at Langton Tower. They had not liked their other haughty neighbour any more than she had and she had been glad of their humorous support, as well as their understanding of her situation. At the time her mother had been trying to match her up with someone she considered more suitable than a working farmer like Samuel Caraford. Tired, angry and at the end of her tether, Rosemary remembered she had been unpardonably rude to her mother and her other guests. Although only seventeen at the time, Ellen Wilshaw had rescued her by suggesting she showed them around the gardens.

'I don't suppose Ellen Wilshaw will remember me after all these years,' she said to Sam, 'but I would like to attend the funeral. It wouldn't do Billy any harm to attend a funeral which is not too closely connected to him either. I think he would have found Liam's a terrible ordeal if he had been able to attend. I shouldn't think the Wilshaws have many friends left in this area after being away so long. They both went to college in Gloucestershire when they left school and they have never actually lived up here since.'

'Mmm, weren't their parents displeased because their daughter insisted on studying the same course as her brother?'

'Yes.' Rosie grinned suddenly. 'I think her mother had even stronger views than mine about what young ladies should do. She thought Ellen should marry a suitable husband and not have a job. Instead she chose a particularly male environment. It was something to do with estate management, I think. I heard later that Ellen Wilshaw had developed a keen interest in valuing and dealing in antiques and she was very good at it. I think the twins were in partnership together. I never heard of either of them being married,' Rosie mused. 'I wonder which of them has the wee girl?'

'No doubt we shall hear eventually but I expect she will arouse some curiosity amongst the locals, poor bairn.'

'Who will arouse curiosity?' Billy asked, coming into the kitchen. His parents explained and asked if he wanted to accompany them and Uncle Alex to the funeral.

'I suppose I could go to represent the third generation of Bengairney Carafords,' he said. 'I can sympathize with the child if she is the object of gossip though. I've had my share of that.'

FIVE

The parish church was surprisingly full by the time the Carafords arrived so they were forced to take seats nearer the front than they would have chosen. There was a mixture of regret, curiosity and genuine sympathy. The laird seemed too young to die and most of the locals regarded him as the last of another county family. There was much craning of scrawny necks when Ellen Wilshaw came in through the vestry at the front of the church. Rosemary sensed at once that her grief was profound at the loss of her twin. Beside her, and almost as tall, was the slim figure of a girl. Billy was surprised. She might not be a woman yet but she was certainly more than a child, even though her honey-gold hair was still worn in a thick plait almost down to her waist. It was clear that both of them had shed tears recently but the faces they presented briefly to the waiting congregation were composed and pale. Billy admired their dignity. Ellen Wilshaw's eyes scanned the sea of faces for a few seconds as she made her way to the seat reserved for them at the front of the church. Her eyes widened slightly in recognition as they met Rosemary's.

After the service the congregation filed past the woman and the girl standing together at the door. Ellen's face looked strained, her thick wavy hair tinged with grey. Rosemary had expected to do no more than murmur her sympathy and pass on with the rest of the congregation but Ellen clasped her hand in both of hers.

'There are refreshments up at the Manor. I hope you will join us there, Rosemary, if you can? You and your – your family?' Her eyes skimmed over Sam, Alex and Billy standing close beside her. It was clear they were all together but Ellen obviously didn't know which of the two men was her husband.

'Very well, thank you, if you're sure?'

'I am sure. It is a relief to see a familiar face.' She gave a strained smile. 'Also I need to speak to the few remaining tenants eventually.' Her eyes moved to Sam and Alex.

Rosemary was surprised again when Ellen and the girl joined their table with a great sigh of relief after circulating around the guests at the other tables set out in the Manor dining room.

'Funerals are never easy, are they?' she said with a wan smile. 'I know one of these fine gentlemen is your husband, Rosemary, but I don't know which one. Presumably you are all tenants on the Scarth Estate?'

'This is Samuel, my husband,' Rosemary introduced them, 'and Alex, my brother-in-law. He farms Bengairney so he is your tenant. Sam and I are at Martinwold. This is our son, Billy. He hopes to farm too but he is going to university in September.'

'Aah, then I would welcome a talk with you, Billy,' Ellen said, summoning a smile. 'Maybe funerals are not the time and place for such things but we don't have a lot of time in Scotland right now so I need to seize every opportunity to make contact and find out what I need to know. Please forgive me. I think you will understand, Rosemary, my grief for my brother is deep and sincere, but for Kimberley's sake I must move on.'

'We all understand, Ellen,' Rosemary said gently. 'I didn't really think you would remember me after all these years, but if there is anything we can do to help....'

'Of course I remember you.' Ellen gave a glimpse of the old mischievous smile Rosemary remembered. 'Trevor and I never forgot when your mother invited us all to that lunch at Langton Tower.' She lowered her voice and glanced across the room. 'And you put our snooty neighbour in his place. We did admire your spirit. I think it was that which helped me stand up to my own parents when they were so opposed to me planning my own future.'

'Gosh, is that Harry Lanshaw?' Rosemary gasped, following her gaze. 'He looks very ... er, portly.'

'He looks an old man, if you ask me,' Ellen said bluntly. 'Fat and bald already. You made a much better choice with Samuel.' She smiled at Sam.

'Thank you, I'm glad you approve,' he said, smiling back at her.

'Indeed I do. Some people have all the luck.' She turned her eyes on Alex. 'Do you have a wife, Mr Caraford?'

'Call me Alex, please, everyone else does, including your brother when he came round for his annual inspection of the farm. And no, I'm not married. I'm a confirmed bachelor. My brother had all the luck when it came to choosing a wife.'

'I see.' Ellen raised her eyebrows. Both Alex and Sam had kept their thick thatch of chestnut-coloured hair and the sprinkling of silver at their sideburns added an air of elegance, especially today, when they were smartly dressed in their dark suits and white shirts. Neither of them ever seemed to put on weight so they looked tanned and fit. Rosie was proud of them.

'It is your son, Billy, whose advice I think we need first,' Ellen went on. 'This is my niece, Kimberley. She is at school in Gloucestershire but I am selling my business down there and both of our houses. I feel we should make a new start. Kimberley agrees, don't you, dear?'

'Yes, I loved coming to Scotland whenever Daddy brought us here for the holidays,' the girl said simply. Rosie guessed she would have her father's and aunt's merry smile when the occasion was not so sad.

'This will mean a change of school. Maybe Billy will tell us about the school he attended and whether he would recommend it?' She looked at Billy. 'Would you have time to call on us one day soon? We need to go back south to wind up our affairs down there but we would appreciate hearing your opinion, Billy. Wouldn't we, dear?'

'Yes. I shall be moving to secondary school,' Kimberley said. 'That will be bad enough, but I'd prefer it if I only need to move once. Although I know it's making everything a rush for Aunt Ellen.' She glanced apologetically at her aunt.

'Don't worry about that, darling. You're all I have now and I shall do everything in my power to make you happy. We both miss your father so much, but he wanted us to be happy and he seemed pleased to know we would be moving back to Scotland, even though we are selling the remainder of the estate.'

'Ah, so Bengairney will be to sell then?' Alex said.

'I'm afraid so, and Highfold. We must have a meeting to discuss things but I would like to settle our affairs in Gloucester first and get Kimberley settled at school up here.'

'That makes sense,' Rosemary said, 'but it might be better if you could both come to Martinwold to talk to Billy. You could come for coffee, or for Sunday lunch if you like? You see, Billy lost part of his left leg in an accident in the summer and he is not driving again yet.'

Billy's mouth tightened and his brows came down in a scowl when Kimberley caught her breath in a gasp. All he wanted was to be normal, but he knew his mother was right, it would be more convenient for them to come to Martinwold. He would never be normal again as far as girls were concerned, he thought dejectedly. That was probably the reason Fenella Lennox had made no effort to see him again. He looked up at the light touch of Kimberley's fingers on the back of his hand.

'That must have been a terrible ordeal, and so painful,' she said softly. 'We didn't know. We don't want to be a nuisance, only....' She chewed her lip. 'I feel quite nervous about going to a larger school and of course I have such a different accent. I suppose some of the girls will mock me for that.'

'The Academy is a mixed school.' He looked at her thick shining hair. 'I guarantee that for every girl who mocks there'll be a boy who admires you.' Billy's own eyes widened as soon as the words were out. The girl was only twelve, for goodness' sake. Whatever had possessed him to speak his thoughts aloud?

'Thank you for saying that. It would be a relief if some of them are friendly.'

'I don't think you need to worry, but I'll ask a few people I know. I'm sure at least one must have a younger sister starting at the Academy after the summer.'

'That would be so good, if I knew even one familiar face.'

So it was arranged that Ellen Wilshaw and her niece would come to lunch the following Sunday before they returned to Gloucestershire. Rosemary was pleased when Alex agreed to join them. It was good to see him and Sam getting back to their old friendly rivalry without the tensions and undercurrents which had spoiled their relationship. Alex would have an opportunity to buy Bengairney now and he admitted he was lucky to be in a position to do so, thanks to the generous price Sam had paid when he bought out his share in Martinwold.

When Sunday came it was even more surprising to both Rosemary and Sam to witness the ease with which Alex and Ellen Wilshaw conversed over lunch. During the conversation it became clear they had already had two meetings at Bengairney since the day of the funeral.

Billy felt almost avuncular towards twelve-year-old Kimberley and he answered her questions patiently. He promised to introduce her to some of the teachers and friends he had known when she and her aunt returned to Scotland.

'Fenella Lennox is still at the Academy so she would have been a good person to show you round and introduce you to people but my family and hers are not in contact anymore,' he said. 'Her brother was my best friend. He was killed in the car accident when I lost my leg.' His mouth tightened. He knew the Lennox household were going through a miserable time but he thought Fenella could have managed to see him somehow, if she had really wanted to. He had a feeling she would not be the first, or the last, girl to cast him aside once they knew he was a cripple. His mother kept telling him he was not a cripple but she didn't know how he felt, or how much Fenella's desertion fretted him.

Rosemary felt embarrassed when Ellen Wilshaw insisted on helping her to carry dishes back to the kitchen and clear away the meal.

'It's a long time since I lived the grand life, Rosemary. Who do you think does it when I'm at home?' Ellen asked with a laugh. 'Anyway, isn't this the time when confidences are exchanged, over the dirty dishes?'

'I suppose it used to be,' Rosemary admitted. 'I have a dishwasher for most of the dishes now and I will leave the roasting tins until later, but you can come and help me make some coffee, if you like,' she added, glancing at Billy and Kimberley, deep in conversation. 'Take Kimberley through to the sitting room, Billy. Do you want coffee now, Sam, or are you and Alex going out for a walk round the animals first?'

'Oh, we'll have a walk round the cows,' they said in unison and everyone laughed.

Once they were alone together in the kitchen, Rosie explained about the earlier estrangement between them and the reason.

'Sam and his family were always so close. I can't tell you how happy it makes me to see them friends again, and I know it will please Tania, tremendously. Tania is their sister, as well as my best friend, so it was often awkward when she invited all of us for a family gathering at Shawlands.'

'You wouldn't believe they'd ever had a wrong word to see them together now,' Ellen said, watching their retreating figures through the kitchen window. 'I really like Alex. We've met a couple of times already and he definitely wants to buy Bengairney as a sitting tenant and he's offered a fair price. That is such a relief. I already have a prospective purchaser for the Manor House provided I agree to sell the Home Farm along with it. The two sales should ease our situation until I settle my own affairs and the proceeds should cover the inheritance tax this time.'

'Will it be a wrench to sell the Manor when it was your family home?' Rosie asked gently.

'Not a bit. It always was a draughty old house and it never had the style and character that your father's house had at Langton Tower. Besides, it costs such a lot to keep up these rambling old mansions these days, between maintenance and heating and council tax, then you need labour. No, I shall have no regrets. I shall sell Highfold Farm too once we're settled up here. Whatever money remains after we've paid the tax man has to be put in trust for Kimberley for her education. Dear Trevor, he was so anxious I should not be out of pocket caring for her, but she is as dear to me as if she were my own child. He made me chief executive and trustee and did everything in his power to make sure she would be in my care but I shall try to adopt her if the authorities will allow a single woman to adopt a teenager.' She grimaced. 'Officials can be so bound by rules they forget about the human elements sometimes.'

'Should I assume Kimberley's mother doesn't...?'

'Fran is dead, but she and Trevor were not married. She was a keen showjumper and really quite splendid. It meant more to her than having a husband or a family. She thought it was a tragedy when she became pregnant. She blamed Trevor, although she was supposed to be on the pill. They had a terrible row. She wanted an abortion, but even her parents opposed that. Almost as soon as Kimberley was born Fran was back in the saddle.'

'How awful,' Rosemary breathed. 'Most mothers love their babies the minute they're born, although I think my mother considered me a bit of a burden, come to think of it.'

'Fran made it clear the child was Trevor's responsibility or she would put her up for adoption,' Ellen said grimly. Trevor and I had bought a house soon after we settled in Gloucestershire and set up our business, but when a house came for sale only a few hundred yards away I bought it for myself. It was a good investment and it meant I was independent if either of us married, but we were still near to each other.' Her voice shook, but she cleared her throat and went on. 'We were so close, Rosemary. I miss him terribly.'

'I'm sure you do,' Rosemary agreed softly.

'Anyway, Francine arranged for a nursemaid to live in when she returned to her horses.'

'A nursemaid? For such a young baby?'

'Yes. She was very young and had no real experience of looking after babies on her own. Trevor asked me to move in with them to supervise her and to avoid any gossip. I'm the nearest Kimberley has had to a mother of her own. Fran was rarely at home and Kimberley was barely two years old when Fran went to South America hoping to buy a horse she considered good enough for the Olympics. She was giving one a trial when she fell off and broke her neck. It sounds cruel to say it, but it was a blessing she was killed. She would have hated to be an invalid. She was so full of energy and plans and ambitions. As a child she was utterly spoiled but she could be very loveable too. It broke her parents' hearts. They moved to the South of France and they have never taken any interest in Kimberley. They're both dead now but Fran had an uncle, her mother's brother. I'm terribly afraid he might try to interfere with Kimberley's care when he hears Trevor has died. He didn't approve of the way Fran's parents ignored their only grandchild because Fran and Trevor were not married.'

'Lots of couples never marry these days,' Rosemary remarked.

'Oh, Trevor wanted to marry Francine, especially when he knew she was pregnant, but she considered marriage was like being in chains and she wanted to be free.'

'So what about your own business, Ellen? What are your plans when you return to Scotland? Or shouldn't I ask?' Rosemary said, her cheeks flushing.

'Of course you can ask. I would so like us to be friends, Rosemary, and I always admired you and the way you managed your own life, instead of allowing your mother to manage it for you as she wanted to do.'

'Oh, she accepted Sam in the end. How could she not? He's so honest and genuine and kind. He's always been a hard worker. We may not be as wealthy as she wanted but we're comfortable and we're happy. Besides, I never loved anyone else.'

'You don't know how lucky you are. I've never met a man I wanted to marry. Before he died it troubled Trevor. He said he and Kimberley had taken up too much of my life, but if I'd really loved someone I'm sure I wouldn't have let anything interfere. I need to respect people who are my friends. I've never met the right man.' She gave a small grin. 'At least not yet.'

'Where do you plan to live when you come back to Scotland if not at the Manor?'

'We shall move into the house where my father's land agent used to live. It's substantial and built of local red sandstone. It has a lot of character. It has been rented out since our father died and Trevor took over the land agent's job himself. Well, there were not enough farms left to merit employing an agent. The house is empty at present. Kimberley prefers it to the Manor House. In some respects she's quite mature for her age. I'm looking forward to redecorating and modernizing parts of it but it's already habitable and it has a large comfortable kitchen which she loves.'

'Home is what you make it,' Rosemary said, pushing the kettle onto the hotplate when she heard Alex and Sam returning.

'I agree. Our partner is buying our share of the business. He has made too good an offer to refuse now he has realized I intend returning to Scotland. He didn't want me to sell to strangers because Trevor and I each owned a third of the company and the buyer would have been the major shareholder. His son will be joining him as an auctioneer and his nephew is a land agent. He admitted I had built up the furniture and antique sales myself and that kept us afloat after the foot and mouth outbreak when cattle sales went down to zero. Like you I'm fairly comfortable financially but I'm not the type to sit around and do nothing. I shall start a new business up here, specializing mainly in antiques. The tenants in Charmwood smallholding are retiring in May. I shall sell the land with vacant possession and keep the buildings. Trevor and I had a good look at them before he became too ill. The barn and two adjoining sheds are stone built. I could convert them into storage and a sale room with adjoining facilities.'

'And of course Charmwood is close to the house where you will be living.'

'Yes, it is. We thought Charmwood Antiques would be quite a good name too. All very convenient if things go according to plan. I do so want to give Kimberley a settled, happy home,' Ellen said with a sigh. 'She has had so many upheavals in her young life. I want to give her security and let her know she is loved.'

'I'm sure she knows that already. It is so clear to us that you adore her and she seems to feel the same about you.'

'I'm all the family she has, really.'

After a lot of consideration, Billy decided travelling on the bus would be one more challenge to overcome. Mounting unfamiliar steps still made him nervous but most of the buses had lower steps these days.

'I could give you a lift to the Academy,' his mother offered as soon as she realized that was where he wanted to go.

'I don't know how long I shall be. I'm planning to talk to Mr Fisher and I promised to find out if any of the folks I knew have younger sisters starting at the Academy for when Kimberley Wilshaw goes there after the summer. They will be returning to Scotland soon.' He sighed. 'Anyway, Mum, my pin leg is never going to go away or grow into a proper leg. I have to try and be a bit more independent before I go off to university in September.'

'Yes, I suppose so, Billy, but do be careful, dear.'

'I will, don't worry, Mum.'

He was surprised that Kimberley's aunt and his mother seemed to be keeping in touch with regular emails since the Wilshaws returned to Gloucestershire and he knew he couldn't let them down. He would have been more surprised to know that Ellen Wilshaw and his Uncle Alex had been in contact even more frequently, and not always to do with business either.

At the Academy, he went first of all to see Mr Fisher, the careers adviser, who had visited him in hospital.

'No, no, sir,' he laughed, 'I haven't come to tell you I've changed my mind about my course in spite of your persuasive arguments. I still want to farm and my parents are coming round to the idea.'

'We're all glad you're alive, Billy, and I'm pleased to see your old spirit returning. You never did let things beat you.'

Billy explained about Kimberley moving to the area and Mr Fisher promised to see what he could discover about next year's intake while Billy went to see some of his old classmates and teachers. He was walking along the corridor towards the exit when a familiar voice called his name.

'Hey, Billy, wait for me, please!' Fenella Lennox hurried towards him. Billy paused warily, but Fenella was smiling broadly. 'You don't know how good it is to see you, Billy. And I'm amazed how fast you're walking, and how erect you are. Mum will be so pleased when I tell her I've seen you.' The shrill ringing of the bell startled them both. 'Drat! I'm supposed to be going to English for the last period. Still, I can skip it for once. Even Mrs Taylor will understand when I tell her I wanted to talk to you while I have the chance.'

'The chance?' Billy repeated coolly, still wary. He was more hurt than he liked to admit that Liam's sister had never been in contact during all the weeks he had been struggling to learn to walk, then back home, trying to do the jobs he had once done so easily. He frowned. 'What do you mean the chance to talk to me? I haven't been for a holiday to the moon.'

'Oh, Billy, I don't blame you for being bitter when your whole life has been turned upside-down, but I'm amazed at how well you're managing. I'm really pleased I've run into you here. Even my father can't prevent me talking to you in school. Shall we go into the prefects room?'

'You said you were going to come to the hospital again? I suppose the sight of a fellow in a wheelchair with a stump of a leg stretched out in front was enough to put you off too,' he said bitterly. Fenella stared at him.

'Some vet I shall make if something like that puts me off,' she scoffed. 'I wanted to visit you, but that day I got a lift with your sister my father had been at the vets and he drove back through the town, instead of along the old by-pass. I don't think he can bear to go down that road since the accident. Anyway, he saw me getting out of Rena's car and he guessed where we had been. I can't tell you how angry he was. When he discovered Mum had known I intended to visit you he ... he flew into a temper and hit her across her face. Then he didn't speak to her for two whole weeks.'

'But why?'

'He–he still thinks it's your fault Derek was killed. He never mentions Liam,' she added bitterly, as they went into the quiet room and she closed the door behind them. 'He can't see that Mum and I are grieving too. Surely in his heart he must know that Derek was to blame, but he refuses to accept it.'

'I see.' Billy frowned. 'It must be hard on your mother being there on her own all day. She never phones my mother now.'

'No, she says it's not worth the risk of him finding out. He's been on the point of striking me a few times recently. He would have done it if Mum hadn't intervened. He hit her instead one of the times and gave her a terrible black eye and a bruised neck.'

'Can't the doctor do anything for him? He never used to be like that.'

'He refuses to see the doctor. Mum got some pills to try to calm him down but he refuses to take them. He said she was trying to poison him. I–I almost dread going home.'

'It certainly sounds a miserable place to be these days,' Billy said slowly.

'It is. I'm desperate to get away to university after fifth year. Mum thinks he has been cracking up ever since Derek started going off the rails. She's afraid he's losing his mind completely.'

'Is it safe for you both to be there with him?' Billy asked in troubled tones.

'I–I don't know. Usually Mum manages to calm him down or distract him. But Miss Wilshaw came to see him before she went back down south. She told him that he would have the opportunity to buy Highfold as a sitting tenant. She obviously believed she was offering him a golden opportunity but he flew off the handle with her too and told her his son had been killed and how dare she come and upset him, and what use was it to him to buy a farm when he hadn't got a son anymore? She tried to explain the advantages to him. She even said he could have a year to think about it because Mr Caraford was already negotiating an early settlement for Bengairney. She thought that would calm him down but the mention of Caraford seemed to set him aflame. He stomped outside without even saying goodbye to Miss Wilshaw. Mum was terribly embarrassed.'

'I'm sure Miss Wilshaw will understand.'

'Mum tried to explain but she already knew about the accident. She said she was terribly sorry for the loss of both of her sons.'

'When she had gone he came in and he unlocked the gun cupboard and took his gun out and started cleaning it. He kept muttering he would shoot the buggers....' Fenella lifted her eyes to Billy's face. She couldn't tell him it was the Caraford name he kept repeating. 'Eventually Mum persuaded him to let her put it back in the cupboard and she locked it and kept the key. When he went to bed she telephoned Doctor Jamieson and told him she was frightened he would use the gun. He telephoned the police. Of course they already knew what he's like and about Derek and – and everything. They came the next day and said they were going round everyone inspecting the gun licences and checking the guns. They told him there was something wrong with his and they would have to take it away to be checked. Mum said he never made a murmur. He just let them take it without protest.'

'That's strange because I remember he used to enjoy going on a pheasant shoot with some of the other neighbours.'

'Yes, he did, but Mum was happier when they took the gun away. He seems to have been calmer since. Not happy calm, you know, but sort of brooding and quiet. He only speaks in monosyllables.'

'It must be very unpleasant,' Billy sympathized. He noticed Fenella never referred to him as Dad now.

'I waited and waited for you to come back for another visit to the hospital, and for you to bring Amanda, but

I think I understand now why you didn't,' he said slowly.

'I thought about writing you a letter to explain but then you might have replied and that would have been awful if he found out. Anyway, why are you here? At school, I mean?' She smiled and he noticed what a transformation it made. Her face was thinner and paler than he remembered and when he looked more closely he saw the strain around her eyes and mouth. He explained about Kimberley Wilshaw moving to a new school and not knowing anyone.

'Oh, I will keep an eye out for her next term.' Then she clapped a hand to her mouth. 'But I shall not be here if I get to university!' She frowned. 'I'll tell you what, though, Billy, I'll find out when the new first years will be coming for their induction days. It should be soon. If she could come then I will show her round myself and introduce her to one or two people I know.'

'Thanks, Fenella. I'm sure she will be grateful. She seems a nice kid, not at all snooty. She's an orphan now that her father has died. That's why they are selling the remains of the estate. Her aunt, Miss Wilshaw, is taking care of her.'

'How awful. Poor girl. At least I have my mum. I shall try not to feel sorry for myself anymore.' She gave him a glimpse of her old smile with the dimples.

'Mr Fisher is making some enquiries too.'

True to his word, Mr Fisher telephoned Martinwold the following afternoon with the names of some of the girls who would be starting at the Academy.

'One of them is the sister of Michael Appleby. Have you arranged for anyone else to share your flat at university yet, Billy?'

'No, I haven't thought about it.' He and Liam had planned to share a flat.

'Then I wonder if you would consider Michael. You do remember him?'

'I know who he is but I don't know him well. He was always quiet, didn't join in much.'

'He works hard at his studies. Things do not come so easily to him as they did to you and Liam Lennox but I believe he will get there. He intends to study biochemistry. His parents are not wealthy but they want to give him and his sister the opportunities they never had, at least as far as they can afford. Michael doesn't want to live in halls either. He can't afford either the time or the money for a hectic social life. After you came to see me it occurred to me the two of you might do very well sharing a flat. I'm sure he will share both the chores and the expenses very fairly. He has a rather dry sense of humour when you get to know him.'

'We could always give it a try,' Billy said slowly. 'I shall need someone to share expenses.'

'I know you have changed, Billy, and that such a near-death experience must make you view things very differently but I hope you will still enjoy your student years, even though you cannot play the sports you enjoyed here at school. There will be the debating society. You were always good at that sort of thing, and you can still sing. How do you plan to get to lectures from your digs? Michael plans to take his cycle to save on bus fares.'

'The flat is fairly convenient. There is a regular bus service but Liam and I had planned to take our bikes too. Now…. Well, my parents are talking of buying an automatic car. Michael may not trust me to drive though, after all the stuff in the papers,' he added bitterly.

'We all know that was a load of rubbish,' Mr Fisher said briskly. 'Try to put it out of your mind and look to the future, Billy. Can I leave you to get in touch with Michael and his sister?'

'Fine, I'll do that. And thanks for the names, sir.'

'Tell your young friend to come to me if she has any problems when she moves here.'

Both Sam and Rosemary were relieved at the prospect of Billy having a steady companion to share a flat with.

'How about me asking Michael and his sister here for tea and inviting Ellen and Kimberley so the two girls can meet on neutral territory?'

'Mrs Wilshaw might not consider the Appleby family suitable company,' Billy said anxiously. 'I mean, them being sort of gentry. Mr Appleby works at the slaughterhouse.'

'I've seen him there,' Sam said. 'He's been there a long time and he's always helpful if anyone needs a hand with a stubborn beast.'

'If Ellen still regarded herself as gentry she would be sending Kimberley to a private school.'

'All the same, you'd better consult them first,' Billy insisted.

Ellen Wilshaw and Kimberley came over the following day. Sam was surprised to see them both dressed in faded jeans, thick polo-neck jumpers and muddy wellingtons, which they both kicked off at the door as though they had been popping in at

Martinwold for years.

'We walked over the fields,' Ellen said, puffing out her cheeks and flinging herself onto a kitchen chair. 'It's further than I thought.'

'Well, the fresh air has certainly brought the colour back to your cheeks.' Rosemary eyed Kimberley and smiled. 'In fact, you're both looking a whole lot better.'

'That's because we have got most of our affairs sorted out down south and we're going to spend the summer making a home up here. Then I shall start converting the Charmwood barn ready for my new enterprise, Charmwood Antiques. We haven't thought of anything better yet. What do you think?'

'It sounds good,' Rosemary said. 'The wood bit fits in with antique furniture.'

'Yes, that's what I thought. Maybe it's a lucky omen,' Ellen said with a smile. She stood up and aimed a playful punch at Billy's chest. 'As for you, young Billy, I'll have you know you're as bad as your Uncle Alex, thinking we're in a different class to ordinary folks. I reckon I've convinced him we're not the snooty snobs you both seem to think. Your mother and I know all about those, don't we, Rosemary?'

'We do indeed, or at least we used to do.'

'Anyway, Billy, I'm pleased you've found someone for Kimberley to meet before she starts at the Academy. We're grateful to you. We would love to meet the boy who will be sharing your flat, and his sister, wouldn't we, Kim?'

'Yes. I expect I'll still be nervous when I first start at a new school but it would be lovely if I knew some-body.'

'In that case,' Rosemary said briskly, 'I'll invite them

for an afternoon. I'm sure Sam will collect them both and I'll take them home later. It will be good for Billy and Michael to have a chance to sort out a few things too.'

'I think Michael has a Saturday job so it would need to be a Sunday. Is that all right?' Billy asked.

'It will suit us fine,' Ellen said. 'I like to hear of young people doing something to help themselves.'

SIX

The Sunday afternoon with the Applebys went well. Billy took Michael to his bedroom where they could talk in peace and Billy was pleasantly surprised to find that Michael was not so quiet when they were alone together. He had very definite views about what he wanted from life and he was prepared to work hard to achieve his goals. They discussed the practicalities of sharing a flat together and both set out their own priorities and boundaries. When they went down to the kitchen for tea, they could hear the two girls in the sitting room laughing and talking. They exchanged satisfied smiles. Billy had already gathered that the Applebys were a close family and he guessed Michael would look out for his young sister whenever possible.

As they entered the kitchen, Billy was surprised to find his Uncle Alex there, chatting to his parents and Ellen Wilshaw. They all seemed perfectly at ease together. The only difference he could see was that Alex was not in his usual clean jeans and sweater. He was wearing smart brown chinos and a suede zipped jerkin. It was open to reveal a cream shirt. He was even wearing a tie.

'You're looking very smart today, Uncle Alex,' he remarked with a wide grin, his green eyes dancing with mischief.

'We–ell, I thought since it was Sunday....' He scowled when both Sam and Billy quirked an eyebrow at him. They knew he didn't usually bother about being smart for them, and Billy didn't think he was out to impress the young Applebys. He glanced at Ellen Wilshaw. She was giving his uncle an admiring look.

'Stop teasing, you two,' Rosemary admonished. 'Alex always looked smart when we were young. He was so fit and light on his feet he could dance every other man off the floor, including big brother Sam.' She cast a teasing glance at her husband.

'Aye, he was always good at the dancing,' Sam agreed, 'and he wasn't bad at the singing either. He used to sing to the cows at the top of his voice while we were milking. I reckon that's where you got your musical talents from, Billy.'

'If you were so good at the dancing, Alex, perhaps you'd agree to partner me for one of the farmers' dances in Dumfries?' Ellen suggested. 'I was going to refuse the invitation. What do you say?'

'It's years since I've been to any of the annual farmers' dances. I think I might be a bit old for that now.'

'Of course you're not too old,' Rosemary said briskly. 'I'll bet you can still show the young folk a thing or two.'

'I feel I ought to put in an appearance,' Ellen said

slowly. 'I wouldn't like to give anyone the impression I think I'm a bit ... well, you know!'

'Too upper class?' Rosemary prompted with a snort of laughter.

'Something like that,' Ellen agreed. 'People do get some strange ideas. Anyway, I need to mix with the local community and make contacts if I'm to build up a new business.'

'What about Kimberley?' Alex asked. 'We can't leave her on her own. It will be a late night.'

'I could ask Mrs Brex if she would stay overnight, I suppose,' Ellen said slowly. It wouldn't be any fun for the poor child with old Brex for company.

'Do you think Kimberley would like to stay overnight with us?' Rosemary asked. 'If the two girls have got on well today, I could invite Mary for the afternoon again so she would have company.'

'Oh, Rosemary, that would be really kind. I know Kim would not relish having Mrs Brex's company for a whole evening.'

'Shout the girls for tea then, Billy,' Rosemary said, 'and Kimberley can let me know what she thinks.'

A fortnight later Kimberley and Mary spent another afternoon together at Martinwold while Ellen Wilshaw went to the dinner dance with Alex. It was a splendid meal and, having lived all his life in the area, Alex seemed to know almost everyone there. He was clearly well respected by his fellow farmers and Ellen liked the way he drew her into the conversation and introduced her to everyone who came up to speak.

'Rosemary was right, Alex, you really are a good dancer,' Ellen said. 'I'm really enjoying myself and if

I'm honest I was rather dreading coming tonight and meeting so many strangers.'

'Rosie used to be a super dancer herself. We won a competition for dancing once,' Alex told her with a smile. 'Sam was jealous as hell.' He grinned, then his expression sobered. 'He needn't have worried because she never had eyes for anyone but him.'

'I can believe that. Would I be right in thinking you would have liked to marry Rosemary yourself?'

'I would have if she'd have had me. I've never looked at another woman.' He paused and held her gaze steadily. 'Until now,' he added softly. Ellen's heartbeat quickened. She had felt attracted to Alex since the first time they met, at her brother's funeral of all places. The attraction had increased as she had got to know him, but until tonight he had given no indication he might feel the same. Surely she was too old to feel like this? Her spirits soared. Alex was good company, they had a lot in common and she enjoyed his sense of humour. Even more importantly, he was kind and considerate and she loved the way he was so patient with Kimberley, answering all her questions and considering her welfare. Kimberley had been more than happy to spend the afternoon and night at Martinwold and meet her new friend again.

It was well after midnight by the time Alex drew the car to a halt at Ellen's home.

'I know it's late, but please come in for a cup of hot chocolate, Alex?'

'Are you sure?' he asked after a momentary hesitation. They both knew that it was not only hot chocolate she was offering.

Much later they lay side by side in Ellen's bedroom,

watching the moonlight making silvery patterns on the walls, and turning the trees to dark silhouettes against the sky.

'I feel as though it's lighting me up too, right from my toes to my head,' Ellen said softly. She hesitated. 'Alex, are you – were you shocked to – to find a woman in her forties still a virgin?' Alex knew she was a capable and confident businesswoman but suddenly she sounded young and insecure. He held her closer, cradling her next to his heart, while his fingers stroked the silky skin of her upper arm.

'Surprised, maybe, because you're a very attractive woman, Ellen, with a lot of style and character, but personally, I am thrilled and delighted to know you have given yourself to me – only to me,' he added softly, his voice deep with passion. 'That's selfish of me, I suppose. I hope you will not regret this tomorrow?'

'Oh no. I've never felt anything like this before. I'm a – I was a virgin by choice. I never met a man I respected enough before, let alone one who aroused so much desire in me. I love Kimberley to bits but I'm pleased she is at Martinwold tonight.'

'Mmm, so am I,' Alex murmured, his fingers moving to stroke the soft creamy skin at her midriff again, moving seductively in ever widening circles. He smiled down at her as she caught her breath and responded eagerly to each caress.

Less than a couple of hours later, Alex opened his eyes, yawned and stretched.

'I have to leave you now, Ellen,' he said softly, with a sigh of regret. 'I need to get home and change then start the milking. I've never felt it was a chore until today.'

'Do you always milk the cows yourself, Alex? I gathered from last night's company that your herd is one of the best in this area and your animals are in demand for breeding far and wide.'

'I've been lucky with the breeding,' he said modestly. 'I have a good man who does the milking every second weekend, or if I am away overnight, but this is my weekend to work. I'm sure Tommy would have taken my turn, especially if he knew the reason,' he added with a grin. 'But I didn't know myself I would be enjoying the best night of my life. Anyway, I don't want to spoil your reputation with gossips like Mrs Brex and my Mrs Walters – at least not yet,' he added more seriously.

'B–but you've no regrets, Alex? Have you?' Ellen asked, still unsure.

'Not one,' Alex assured her. 'Well, maybe one,' he teased, his eyes dancing as he looked down into her wide eyes. 'I regret that I have to leave you and that I shall have to sleep alone in my own bed tonight.'

'Oh, Alex! You are a tease, but I share that particular regret and I don't know when we shall have an opportunity like this again with Kim around.'

'No, that may not be so easy,' Alex agreed. 'We'll not rush into anything, but we're both adults and old enough to know what we want. Give Kim time to get used to us being together. Bring her to Bengairney often. She seems to like the farm and the animals. She's a sensible lassie, but I would hate to upset her if she thought I was taking you away from her, especially when she has just lost her father, poor lassie. When you think she might accept you marrying me, and living at Bengairney, then let me know. That is if you think you might consider marriage, Ellen?' She heard the diffidence in his tone.

'I would marry you tomorrow, Alex,' she said softly, 'if we only had ourselves to consider.'

'You would?' He leaned down and hugged her tightly, kissing her with a passion which made the blood sing in her veins. He groaned. 'If I don't go right now I think the cows will still be waiting to be milked at midday.'

At Martinwold Billy faced Kimberley across the breakfast table and grinned.

'I'll bet your aunt will be tired out and needing a long lie in bed this morning after a night of dancing with Uncle Alex, at least if what Mum says about him is true. It will probably be lunchtime before she comes to pick you up. Would you like to come for a walk round the animals, see the young calves and such like?'

'I'd love that, if you're sure? I mean, is it all right for you to – to walk much?' As soon as the words were out Kim saw him scowl and knew she had said the wrong thing. She had already gathered he was sensitive about losing his leg and being unable to play the sports and other things he used to do. She flushed painfully. 'I'm sorry. I've seen for myself that you're determined to do most of the things we all do. I–I didn't mean to – to....'

'Forget it,' Billy said brusquely. 'I shall have to get used to people treating me differently, I suppose. Can you swim?'

'Swim?' Kim was flummoxed by the sudden change of topic. 'I can swim but I'm not wonderful.'

'Mmm, it's a pity we didn't tell you to bring your swimming costume. At least I can still do that and I've proved I can travel on the bus without help. Liam and I often went swimming, and Fenella, his sister, usually came too. Fen swims like a fish but she's not even allowed to speak to me now, let alone meet up. Her father blames me for the accident. So remember to bring your swim things next time you come to stay.' Listening to them while she watched the toast, Rosemary's heart ached for her son. He sounded like a small boy desperate to prove he could do the same as his friends.

'Well, I suppose I could b–but ... I don't know ...' Kim broke off hesitantly.

'You afraid you might freak out if you have to see my stump, is that it?' Billy asked harshly. 'I suppose most girls will feel like that.'

'It would take more than that to freak me out, as you put it,' Kim said, surprising him with her impatient tone. 'I meant I don't know if I shall be invited to stay here again. It was very good of your parents to have me but ...'

'Oh, Kimberley, I have loved having you to stay,' Rosemary said, coming across to the table with the toast rack. 'You're welcome to come any time. I miss having my own girls at home and it's good for Billy to have young company.' She glanced at his frowning face. 'You'll have to excuse him if he's a bit touchy about his leg, or the sight of his stump. You don't strike me as the type of girl who gets squeamish easily.'

'I'm not.'

'The doctors say Billy has done well to gain his

balance and learn to walk so well. He has an advantage with being young and he has strength in his arms and shoulders from playing rugby and working on the farm. It takes most patients about three months in rehabilitation but they allowed Billy to come home only eight weeks after the accident.'

'That is very good, and swimming will be good exercise without pressure on the legs, I suppose. I'd like to go swimming with you, Billy, but it will depend on what Aunt Ellen wants me to do. She didn't used to go out much in the evenings, except for her work.' Billy thought she sounded a bit lost and lonely and he was sorry he had snapped at her. After all, she was only twelve. It was easy to forget that. She was as tall as his mother and not at all like the giggly girls he remembered in their first year at the Academy.

'Would you mind if Ellen did want to go out more now she has come to live up here again?' Rosemary asked gently.

'No. It is what Daddy wanted. One of the last things he said was that we had taken up too much of Aunt Ellen's life already. He said she will be lonely when I'm older and want to go away or have a career and he wanted me to have a happy life of my own choosing. He said the best thing would be if Aunt Ellen found a nice man and got married so that she would always have a companion. He said I must not mind if she did that. Of course I wouldn't mind if it made her happy, especially when I know it is what Daddy wanted. She misses him as much as I do, but I hope she chooses a nice man. Maybe somebody like Mr Caraford.'

'Uncle Alex?' Billy chuckled. 'It's a pity he's a confirmed old bachelor.'

'Hey, not so much of the old, Billy,' his mother admonished.

'I wouldn't like to stay on my own in that big house without any neighbours or anything, though, if Aunt Ellen does start going out at nights.' Kimberley wrinkled her nose slightly. 'It will not be much fun having Mrs Brex to stay either, but I shall try to remember Daddy would have wanted me to fit in.'

Rosemary put an arm round her shoulders, giving her an affectionate hug.

'You're a good lassie, Kimberley. Any time you think your Aunt Ellen wants to go out for an evening, promise you will phone and tell me. I will keep Rena's wee room ready for you and you can come whenever you want.'

'Can I really?' Kimberley looked up at her, her blue eyes shining. 'I would much prefer that,' she said with feeling. Then, 'Daddy and my friends and teachers called me Kim. I prefer that really. It – it makes me feel I belong. I told Mary that and she's going to call me Kim.'

'Then we shall call you Kim too,' Rosemary said with a smile. 'Isn't that right, Billy?'

'Whatever you say,' Billy said. 'What's in a name? It's the person that counts. So are you coming with me for a look round the animals?'

'Yes, I'd love to do that.'

'You can borrow my wellingtons, Kim,' Rosemary said.

'Thank you. I will bring my own if I do come again.'

Billy was pleased that Kim showed a keen interest in the animals and asked intelligent questions about their feed and their health. She asked why they all had two big ear tags. He explained that it was a government regulation and even if they died, or went for slaughter, they still had to have their own number and a record of it had to be sent to the government offices.

'It is since the BSE outbreak so that every animal can be traced. I believe there are more records for cattle than there are for humans now. Come on and we'll walk up the field so you can see the heifers. They are carrying their first calf so we need to check them every day.' He looked at her out of the corner of his eye to see if she knew what he was talking about but she merely nodded.

'Your Uncle Alex explained a bit about that and about choosing semen from different bulls for his breeding programme when he needs a new blood line, and about using artificial insemination. It sounded quite interesting. I shall have to wait and see how I get on at school but if Aunt Ellen insists I must go to university I thought I might like to study animal genetics.'

'Really? I'm amazed at Uncle Alex telling you all that – about his breeding programme, I mean.'

'Well, I did ask him, and I'm not a child, you know.'

'If you say so,' Billy teased. 'Actually, it's hard to remember you're only twelve. I suppose you've had more trouble in your life than most girls your age. It has made you more serious and mature.'

'Tell me about your friend, the one who died. Mary Appleby says he was brilliant at school. Her brother told her he wanted to be a doctor.'

Amazingly Billy found himself telling her about Liam and the things they had done together and how much he missed his friendship. When she asked about the accident, he found himself telling her details he had never spoken of before, including how afraid he had been just before it happened. He told her about some of his experiences in the hospital too, things he had never mentioned to anyone else.

It was after eleven when Ellen Wilshaw telephoned to apologize for leaving Kimberley so long.

'Don't worry about her, Ellen. She and Billy have gone for a walk together. You may as well join us for dinner when you collect her. I'll have it ready by 12.30.'

'Well, if you're sure you don't mind.'

'Of course not. And by the way Kimberley has asked us to call her Kim. She says her friends all called her that. Do you mind?'

'Mind? Of course not. Trevor often called her Kim, too. Kimberley was her mother's choice of name. I didn't know she had a preference.'

As soon as Ellen put the phone down, Rosemary dialled the Bengairney number. There was no reply so she tried Alex's mobile. He answered immediately.

'I didn't think you'd feel like cooking Sunday lunch after having a late night, Alex,' Rosemary said with laughter in her voice. 'Come over and join us and tell us all about your evening and the local gossip.'

'What gossip?' Alex asked sharply, his heartbeat quickening. Surely he and Ellen had not caused any gossip yet?

'I don't know what gossip,' Rosemary chuckled. 'But there's usually some. Anyway, Kim is still here. Ellen is collecting her soon and they'll be staying for lunch so you may as well join us, unless a night's dancing tires you out these days?' she added with a mischievous laugh.

'Dancing never tired me out, as you should know. As a matter of fact the evening made me feel like a spring chicken again so I'll be with you for lunch. And thanks, Rosemary. I'll see you in a wee while.' Rosemary nodded to herself, a small smile lifting the corners of her mouth. Alex sounded on top of the world. If there was a spark of attraction between Alex and Ellen Wilshaw, there was no harm in helping it along a little.

SEVEN

True to her promise, Fenella Lennox kept a special lookout for Kim on induction day when the new year's students came to look around the school. She was patient and thorough, answering her and Mary Appleby's questions and giving them advice about the quirks of the various teachers and how to cope with the dinner queues, but she couldn't quite dispel the feeling of embarrassment when she recalled how nasty her father had been to Kim's aunt and it made her a little stiff and awkward when she addressed Kim directly. When she showed them where the toilet block was, Mary asked if new pupils still got bullied by the older girls in there.

'Oh no, there should not be any bullying anywhere in school,' Fenella declared.

'If there is bullying, I expect I shall be one of those they pick on.' Kim grimaced. 'I have only to speak for them to realize I'm different and a newcomer to this area.' Fenella frowned as she looked at their anxious faces. Kim had sensed a reserve in the older girl's manner when she was addressing her personally, and it was not there with Mary. She wondered if Fenella resented her because her father had been their landlord, or maybe because Aunt Ellen was friendly with Rosemary Caraford and her family and that included Billy. After all, he and Fenella did seem to be special friends. He had said she could swim like a fish, and he had asked her to look out for her today. It never occurred to her that Fenella's reserve towards her was on account of Syd Lennox and the shame she felt after his obnoxious behaviour towards Ellen Wilshaw when she had called to discuss the tenancy.

'Come with me,' Fenella said now, as though reaching a decision. 'I will show you Mrs Burgess's room and introduce you both if she is in. If you have the slightest hint of bullying she would want to know and she would deal with it tactfully, without involving you personally. We did have a group of girls who were bullies two years ago and she dealt with them.'

Later that evening, Mary was full of praise for Fenella Lennox as she ate her evening meal with her parents and brother. The following day Michael made a point of seeking out Fenella and thanked her for her kindness to his young sister and her friend Kim. Fenella looked up at him, her eyes widening in surprise. She felt warmed by his praise.

'It was no trouble. I had Liam to look out for me when I moved schools, but you will have moved on?'

'Yes, as a matter of fact I shall be taking Liam's place and sharing a flat with Billy Caraford. I hope you don't mind?'

'Of course not. Billy will need somebody and we both miss Liam terribly.' Her voice croaked and Michael reached out and put a gentle hand on her arm.

'I understand,' he said simply and Fenella saw the sincerity in his brown eyes. After that the two of them often stopped for a chat if they happened to be having dinner at the same time, or when they met in the library. Fenella wondered why she had never noticed Michael before, but then she had not paid much attention to the older boys, except for Liam and Billy and their close friends. She found herself telling him about Liam and their home life and eventually she confided her worries about her father's mental state and how frightened she was in case he injured her mother more seriously. Michael was a good listener. He had already heard about Syd Lennox's irrational behaviour from his father. The man had caused trouble when he delivered some bullocks to the slaughterhouse but he did not tell Fenella that.

Kim settled in at the Academy better than Ellen had dared to hope, reassuring her that her decision to move back to Scotland had been good for both of them. Mary Appleby was proving to be a true friend. In spite of the difference in their backgrounds the two girls got on well and had a lot in common, including a determination to do their best at school. Ellen offered a silent thank you to Billy for introducing her niece to Mary, as well as to other first-year pupils. He was a thoroughly nice young man, even if he did sometimes withdraw into some dark world of his own. Considering his life-changing experiences of the past year, she felt that was understandable.

Billy and Michael Appleby started at university and

embarked on a new phase in their lives too. Sam had bought an automatic car for Billy but neither he nor Rosemary could resist issuing several admonitions to drive carefully.

'Don't worry so much,' Billy said irritably. 'Anyone would think the crash was my fault. I am careful and I intend to come home once a fortnight to take my turn with the relief milking.' Gradually he was learning to accept that some things he had once taken for granted were difficult, if not impossible, but they often made him irritable and even depressed.

'An extra pair of hands for the milking is always welcome,' Sam said, 'but we expect you to make the most of your time at university, both with work and pleasure.' He was also learning to accept when Billy offered to help. One of the doctors had explained that the psychological effects of losing a limb were often as devastating as the physical ones and if Billy wanted to attempt things they should encourage him to have a go.

Rosemary could scarcely believe a year had passed since the accident. She rarely heard from Jane Lennox but she knew from the talk on the country grapevine that Mr Lennox was getting even more difficult to live with and he still refused to accept Derek's death, and his part in the crash. Fenella had done exception- ally well in her school examinations and was starting university a year earlier than usual. Several of the sales representatives, who called at both farms, were convinced Sydney Lennox had driven her away from home with his foul temper and irrational outbursts.

Ellen Wilshaw was finding him impossible to deal with as a tenant of the Scarth Estate. She had given him a year from her brother's death to decide whether he wanted to buy his farm as a sitting tenant, or retire and give up the tenancy. The general opinion was that he would be foolish to miss the opportunity to buy Highfold, even if he had to borrow the money. He could make a good profit if he sold it with vacant possession. He simply refused to commit himself, or to discuss his plans, and meanwhile fences and buildings were deteriorating for want of maintenance. Ellen had been to see him twice recently and both times he had walked away, muttering and swearing to himself.

'His wife apologized profusely,' Ellen said to Rosemary. 'She seems a nice person but God knows how she puts up with such a boor of a man. He's not normal if you ask me. I shall have to see our solicitor and ask him to write Mr Lennox a letter, giving him a deadline. Otherwise I don't believe he'll ever reach a decision. I can't tell you how grateful I am to Alex for buying Bengairney, and settling up so quickly. He's been able to advise me on lots of other things too. It has been such a help with sorting out Trevor's affairs, and of course they affect Kim too.'

'Speaking of Alex, how are the two of you getting on?' Rosemary asked, her blue eyes dancing with mischief. 'Sam said you had been at the market with him and you were helping him wash and groom his heifers ready for the sale as though you'd been doing it all your life.'

'It's not so very different to grooming ponies for a show and I did plenty of that when we were young. I really enjoyed the day. Alex is so good at explaining what needs to be done and why. He's very good company, Rosie. I never imagined I could be this happy and content after Trevor died, but the year has gone so quickly.'

'Mmm, we've noticed Alex seems to have a permanent smile on his face these days,' Rosie teased. Ellen blushed. Since the night of the dinner dance she and Alex had spent several very pleasant afternoons together, both at Charmwood and at Bengairney, but they were both aware their respective housekeepers were insatiable gossips so they tried to be discreet.

'Kim likes Alex and I think children have an instinct about these things. He's very patient with her. He's even teaching her to milk when she's there at the weekends.'

'We think both you and Kim have been very good for Alex. He used to be wonderful with our three children, at least until he and Sam quarrelled. You have restored him to the humorous, good-natured man he used to be.'

'You think so? Then I'm glad. I've been very grateful for the nights you have had Kim to stay. It has given us an opportunity to be alone together and get to know each other better. I would like to ask you an even bigger favour, Rosemary,' Ellen added diffidently.

'Ask away. I can always refuse.'

'I – we – we wondered whether you would mind having Kim to stay for a long weekend? I would like to accompany Alex to a pedigree sale down south in about a month's time. That will be nearly Christmas.' Ellen's colour had deepened in spite of her efforts to appear nonchalant.

'Of course we wouldn't mind having Kim to stay. She could get the bus to school from here. It will be no problem. You and Alex go ahead and make your arrangements.'

Arrangements? Ellen caught her breath. Had Rosie guessed what they were planning?

Jane Lennox had bought a flat in Glasgow, using the money from her first husband's life insurance. Fenella would be there for several years and she felt it would be a good investment, especially if they let one room to a fellow student to help with overhead expenses. Fenella felt a sense of release to be away from Syd Lennox and his moods. She enjoyed her studies and she was happier than she had thought possible after Liam's death, especially since she had found such an understanding friend in Michael Appleby. They kept in regular contact by email, exchanging news, sharing problems and simply enjoying discussions together.

'It's such a relief to be away from home and his sudden outbursts of temper,' she told her mother on the telephone. 'Couldn't you make an excuse to do some Christmas shopping, Mum, and come for a weekend? Joanne goes home every third weekend so we could arrange it for when she's away. It would be lovely with just the two of us.'

'Christmas?' Jane Lomax sighed heavily. 'I can hardly believe it's that time again. It would be lovely to see you, Fen, and to get away from here for a couple of nights. I'll see what I can do.'

As it happened, Ellen and Alex were away the same weekend that Jane planned to stay in Glasgow. Billy had finished lectures and brought work home with him for the Christmas holidays. He was surprised at how pleased he felt when he discovered Kim was staying at Martinwold for four nights.

'Your mother said you were due home, Billy, so I brought my swimsuit in case we go swimming again.'

'That's good, but I must take my turn at the milking and keep my hand in if I'm going to farm. Anyway, I need to earn some money, you know.'

'I could get up early and help you,' Kim offered eagerly. She was offended when Billy threw back his head and laughed aloud. Her cheeks burned and her blue eyes sparked angrily. 'What's so funny about that?' she snapped.

'You are. You wouldn't know which end of the cow to put the teat-cups on.' Rosemary had entered the kitchen in time to hear the end of the conversation and she bit back a smile of amusement. Billy was going to get the come-uppance he deserved, she thought. She had heard Alex telling Sam how Kim helped with the cows whenever she was at Bengairney. He had been impressed at the speed with which she had learned to milk, but he was even more delighted that she was beginning to recognize the cows by name and asking questions about their pedigrees. Rosie knew Kim was both intelligent and practical, as well as observant, and she was not without spirit now she knew them all better.

'Do you want to bet?' she challenged Billy now.

'Nice girls don't bet.'

'I can't help being a girl and I never pretended to be nice. That's just a label you think should fit me because my father was the laird around here. I'll bet you the entry money to the swimming baths that I can put a milking unit on a cow as quickly as you can.'

'I may have only one leg but I still have two good arms and I'm pretty good at milking, I'll have you know. Still want to bet?' Billy looked at her keenly. 'How do you know you'll be able to reach? We stand in a pit, you know.'

'I've seen it. So is it a bet?'

'OK. If I win you pay me into the swimming. And give me a kiss,' he added, a devilish light appearing in his green eyes. Both Rosemary and Kim's eyes widened at Billy's audacious suggestion. Kim blushed a little but she was determined not to give in. She had never kissed a boy yet but that didn't stop her having teenage fantasies.

'I think I'm safe. It's a bet.'

As it turned out, Billy was astonished at how quick and efficient Kim was in the parlour. She was tall for her age and could reach the cows more easily than his mother. He had been so sure he would beat her easily, he didn't even pretend to hurry. He opened his mouth in surprise and Kim laughed aloud at his expression.

'So, Billy Caraford, you owe me. You have to pay me into the swimming baths.'

'I concede defeat,' Billy said. 'I will pay you in, as well as giving you a kiss.' He loved to see the ready colour spring to her cheeks. She was so young and fresh. 'But you cheated.'

'Cheated?' Kim squeaked indignantly. 'How could I cheat with something like this?'

'Someone has been teaching you and you didn't tell me. No wonder Mother was smiling. She knew you would win, didn't she?'

'Your Uncle Alex lets me help him in the milking

parlour when I'm at Bengairney. I love everything about that place; the house is so homely, and I love the farm. He's teaching me the names of all the cows and I'm learning some of the pedigrees. He even let me help him with his records one weekend.'

'He did?' Billy was amazed both at her eagerness to help and his uncle's willingness to encourage her, considering he was such a keen breeder. 'I reckon you and your mother have changed Uncle Alex. He even looks younger and he's like he used to be when I was little, always teasing and having a bit of a laugh.'

'He's nice. Aunt Ellen and I both think so. In fact, Aunt Ellen says, except for Daddy, he's the nicest man she's ever met.'

When the milking was finished, Billy and Kim were ravenous for breakfast. They both grabbed for the last slice of toast amidst a burst of laughter, which gladdened Rosemary's heart. A year ago she had almost despaired of ever seeing Billy laugh again.

'If the pair of you eat much more you'll sink like bricks in the swimming pool,' she teased.

'Kim sinks like a brick anyway,' Billy laughed. Secretly he had been delighted to find he could still swim so much better than she could.

'I do not sink!' Kim said indignantly. 'Even if I can't do the crawl like you can or swim like a fish, like your girlfriend, it doesn't ...'

'Which girlfriend?' Billy demanded with a scowl. He avoided most of the girls at university. Both he and Michael had been dismayed at the way a lot of the girls slept around as readily as they kissed goodnight. Billy had lost a lot of his confidence around girls since the accident. He never attempted to dance and he had never enjoyed much alcohol. He was even more wary of getting drunk now. In these respects he and Michael Appleby were well suited. 'Which girlfriend?' he repeated, wondering if Michael's young sister had mentioned the three Indian girls who frequently visited their flat.

'I don't know how many you've got but you told me yourself that Fenella Lennox could swim like a fish.'

'Well, so she can, but then Fen and Liam seemed to excel at most things.'

'I see,' Kim muttered. 'I'm going to get changed.'

Later she covered the lengths of the baths in her own steady breaststroke while Billy gave himself an exhilarating workout. It was the crawl he enjoyed most, especially now. At university he often went to the gym to keep up the strength of his shoulders and upper body as the physiotherapist at the hospital had advised. He rested at the end of the swimming baths, waiting for Kim to reach him. It was still early and there weren't many others in the pool.

'You're very good for my morale, Kim,' he said with a grin when she joined him.

'What do you mean by that?' she demanded. Billy frowned. It was not like Kim to be short with him and she had been unusually quiet on the way into town. He had never seen her moody before. He didn't know what he had said or done to make her this way.

'What do I mean? Just that swimming is still something I can do well. If you had been competitive like Liam or Fen I'm not sure that I would have risked coming with you. Come on, we'll do another couple of lengths at a nice leisurely pace before we get out, eh?'

'All right.' Kim smiled suddenly. Billy smiled back,

relieved. It was like the sun breaking through the clouds. His twin sisters and his Ritchie cousins were all much older than him and he rather liked having a sort of adopted younger sister. Even the first time they had come swimming together she had not flinched at the sight of his stump. In fact she had asked if she could touch it and her fingers had stroked it gently. 'Pleased to meet you, Charlie,' she had said with a wide grin and given it a little pat. Between the two of them, his stump was always referred to as Charlie now. She was quick to notice when he had been doing something which caused discomfort. Then she would ask, 'Is Charlie hurting today?' She never made him feel like a freak and he wondered whether Fenella would really be as phlegmatic, for all her tough words about being a vet and needing to see all sorts of wounds. After all, he was a human being, not one of her animals. She would soon be home for the Christmas holidays too but he doubted whether she would risk coming to see him and he knew he couldn't go over to Highfold while her father still bore him a grudge.

Kim was helping clear away after their Sunday lunch when the telephone rang.

'I'll get it,' Sam called from the hall, then, 'It's for you Kim. It's your Aunt Ellen.'

'Oh, I wonder if something's wrong. They're not due back until tomorrow evening.' She disappeared into the hall. Rosemary and Billy heard her sudden whoop of delight and their eyes widened. Kim was usually very composed for a teenager. She had left the hall door open and they could hear her chattering and asking questions but they had no idea what about.

'You'll never guess what Aunt Ellen has done!' she said, bounding back into the kitchen. She stopped short and her expression sobered. 'I do hope you will be as pleased as I am. They've got married at a register office. They wanted me to be the first to know. Isn't it exciting? We're going to move our stuff to Bengairney and live there, all the time.'

'Oh, Kim! I am every bit as delighted as you are,' Rosemary said warmly. 'I think they were attracted the first time they met. I am so very happy for them, and I'm pleased you are happy too. I know Alex will be good and kind to both of you.'

'That's exactly what Daddy wished for Aunt Ellen – a good, kind man as a companion. Isn't it wonderful!' She did a little dance around the kitchen table.

'Billy, go into the room and tell your father the news,' Rosemary said, smiling broadly.

'Oh, I nearly forgot. Uncle Alex is going to telephone tonight to speak to both of you. I think they would like to stay away another two nights, if it's all right for me to stay longer?'

'Of course it's all right, Kim. You're welcome to stay as long as you like. This will be your last week at school, I think? Before the Christmas holidays begin, I mean.'

'It's the last full week and three days next week.' She sent Billy a mischievous glance. 'It's only lazy university students who get long holidays.'

'I'll have you know, young Kim, I have worked hard this term and I've finished early. Most of them will not be home until the end of next week.'

'Aunt Ellen says we shall spend the holidays moving

our stuff to Bengairney. I'm so excited,' she laughed, doing another little dance around the kitchen with the remaining dishes.

'I wonder if Ellen intends to sell your present house now then?' Rosemary pondered.

'I asked her that but she said she will keep it for now. Uncle Alex has had a brilliant idea.'

'Alex has?'

'Yes. He suggests she furnish the lounge and dining room and the main entrance hall to show how elegant her antique pieces of furniture could look in some-one's home. We have carpets and some polished floors already and she could leave most of the light fittings so it will look good. It will be easy to move pieces around when some are sold or when Aunt Ellen buys new items. She is aiming at building up a name for quality.'

'It doesn't sound as though Uncle Alex minds having a wife with a separate business of her own?' Billy remarked.

'They have obviously discussed it if it was Alex's idea to use the house as a setting for antiques instead of doing up the barns as a showroom. Ellen will have the upstairs for her own use and office space, and she'll have the kitchen and toilet facilities to herself when she's there at meal times. It sounds ideal. Alex is used to running his own business. He will be more than happy to have the bonus of a wife and family, with Ellen and Kim, living at Bengairney.'

'I don't think I would want my wife to have a business of her own. I'd want her to help me, like you help Dad.'

'You're a young chauvinist, Billy. You may have to

change your ideas if you get a career girl like Fenella Lennox for a wife. Anyway, I kept on my own business, running the gardens up at Langton Tower, when your father and I were first married. I had to give up when the twins were born, of course, but I still did the accounts and kept my share of the partnership until I passed it on to Rena.'

'I didn't know you still worked at the garden centre after you married Dad.'

'It was before you were born. I've always been here for you, and spoiled you no doubt.' She turned to Kim. 'I'm going to phone Alex's sister, Tania. She will be as pleased by this news as we are. I think we must make a celebration meal for Tuesday evening for when they come home. Do you think they would like that?'

'Oh yes! I think it's a super idea. Can I help?' Her eyes shone with excitement. 'I do wish I didn't need to go to school. Maybe I could bake this afternoon? I can make chocolate cake and Swiss rolls and shortbread. Or – or did you mean to do something else?' she asked diffidently. 'I mean, more like dinner?'

'I'll phone Tania and then we'll decide between the three of us,' Rosemary said. 'If we decide on dinner maybe you could make a pudding, Kim?'

'I know how to make a good trifle. At least Daddy said it was good, but I'd need to wait until after school for that....' Her face fell with disappointment. 'I can make cheesecake, and lemon duchess, and I love chocolate and cherry gateau, but we would need to shop for the ingredients, I suppose? I'd love to do something to let them know how happy I am for them.'

'We'll think of something, Kim,' Rosemary said warmly, and gave her a hug.

'We shall be able to give old Jim, the postie, a bit of news for once,' Billy said gleefully. 'He always knows what's going on before everyone else. I'll give you a lift to school on Monday so you don't need to leave so early, Kim, then you can see his face when you tell him.'

'All right.' She nodded and gave a conspiratorial grin. It was the first time in her life she had had anyone young to share her thoughts and plans and Billy was a lot more patient than she had expected after their first meeting at her father's funeral. He was also a lot more sensitive about his disability than she had first realized. Although she was six years younger than he was, she felt strangely protective over that.

On Monday morning Kim was dressed in her school uniform and had her books packed ready to leave when they saw Jim and his red post van turning into the farmyard.

'It's time we were leaving, but watch his face when we tell him the news,' Billy whispered, pulling open the door before the postman even had time for his usual rat-tat-tat. 'Good morning, Jim. We've got news for you for once. Tell him, Kim.'

'B–but you can't have heard already!' Jim gasped hoarsely. 'They only found him this morning. The police are there now. It can't have got round the parish yet....'

Billy and Kim drew back, staring at him, noticing his unusual pallor. His eyes were not crinkling with laughter today. They looked dull with shock.

'Come in, Jim,' Rosemary said, looking over the shoulders of Billy and Kim. She sensed at once that something had shaken the elderly postman. 'You look as though you could do with a seat and a cup of tea. Has something upset you?'

'It's the shock. Suicide! I never thought he'd do that. Well, I know the man hasna been himsel' for a long time, but....' He shook his grey head in bewilderment. 'I never thought he'd take his own life.'

'Wh–who are you talking about?' Rosemary asked, pouring boiling water into the teapot and pushing the milk and sugar closer to Jim. She saw his hands were shaking.

'Highfold. Mrs Lennox is in Glasgow, visiting her lassie this weekend. A terrible black eye she had on Friday morning.'

'Do you mean Syd Lennox? Has he...?'

'Aye. The lad who works for him couldna get any reply so he got the other man. He was dead when they found him. The police are there. I left the letters and came on here.'

'He's taken his own life?' Rosemary repeated. She was stunned. It took courage to do something like that, either that or the deepest despair. She glanced up. 'It's time you were on your way, Billy, or Kim will be late for school. I–I don't think either of you should mention this until we're sure about, well, sure what has happened.' They both nodded, subdued, their young faces filled with dismay, unable to take in the news. Suicide. It was such a final step to take. In that moment Billy forgot all the recent bitterness and distress Syd Lennox had caused. He remembered the hard-working kindly man he had been when he and Liam were young boys. This sort of thing only happened in other communities, to other people, to strangers. Kim had never met the man but she knew Aunt Ellen had had trouble with him and she sensed the effect his death was having on Billy and his mother. She shivered.

Rosemary and Kim had made a delicious meal for Alex and Ellen's return. Rena and her family had come down to join the celebration as well as Tania and her husband, Struan Ritchie, and Billy's cousins, Christine and Steve. They were older than Billy but neither of them were married yet. Kim was tall and mature for her age and Steve flirted outrageously with her. 'Can't you see you're embarrassing her?' Billy hissed, angrily. 'She's too young for your usual flirting.'

'You wouldn't be jealous, Cousin Billy? Or would you?' Steve teased, cocking an eyebrow at him. 'Mind you, I don't blame you. She'll be a stunner in another couple of years.' Billy glowered at him, relieved when Uncle Alex and his new bride arrived and distracted everyone's attention. Irrepressible as always, Steve couldn't resist commenting.

'Uncle Alex always said he was a confirmed bachelor. Now here he is, acting like a schoolboy in love. He even looks ten years younger. Marriage must agree with him, eh? Our new Aunt Ellen isn't half bad either.'

'No, she's not. She's a very nice person,' Billy said. 'I expect your mother will be inviting them to your house, especially now Dad and Uncle Alex are good friends again.'

The meal went well but Alex had always been sensitive to atmosphere and several times he was aware of glances being exchanged or topics of conversation changed, especially between Rosemary, Sam and Tania. It irritated him and made him wary.

'I'll bring the coffee through to the sitting room,' Rosemary said at one point, standing up. Alex frowned, aware that she had interrupted the conversation deliberately. He stood up quickly.

'Before you move, Ellen and I would like to thank you for a delicious meal to welcome us home, but if there's one thing I never could stand it's insincerity. I can sense the undercurrents. I can't help it if you don't approve of us getting married, or of the way we have done it in private. This is the way we wanted it. Ellen has made me happier than I ever believed possible. So if any of you have something to say, for God's sake get it off your chests and say it – not that I think our marriage has anything to do with any of you, except perhaps Kim, and I believe her congratulations are genuine.' He watched Rosemary and Sam exchange the inevitable speaking glance. 'Well?' he demanded.

'We're all delighted you and Ellen are married,' Sam said, clearing his throat. 'We're pleased to see you both looking so happy. If you do sense an undercurrent, then I'm sorry, but it has nothing to do with your marriage. We're as pleased about it as you are yourselves.'

'But there is something then?' Ellen asked. 'I sensed something wasn't right too.'

'Oh, Aunt Ellen, everyone is happy you and Uncle Alex have got married,' Kim cried, seeing the sheen of tears in the eyes of her beloved aunt. 'It's the awful news about Mr Lennox committing suicide that spoiled everything. We didn't want to tell you yet. Aunt Rosemary thought it might cast a shadow so we all agreed not to mention it until tomorrow.'

Alex stared at her then sat down with a gasp.

'Sydney Lennox has committed suicide? That's certainly not pleasant news to come home to. Still, I'm relieved to know the atmosphere is not disapproval of our marriage.'

'Of course not, never that, old man,' Sam said, getting up and clapping him on the back. 'Come on through to the room and we'll try to put the news about Syd Lennox aside for tonight.'

'No, you were right,' Alex said, noticing his wife's pale face. 'You look shocked, Ellen.'

'I am. Mr Lennox would get the letter from our solicitor on Saturday morning,' she said in a low voice, her blue eyes deeply troubled. 'It was a final reminder asking for his decision about Highfold. It was probably the last straw. Supposing he was incapable of making a decision? My letter may have pushed him over the edge. Oh Alex, I couldn't bear it if he took his life because of anything I have done.'

'I don't think anyone really knows what made him do it,' Rosemary said quietly. 'Sam and I went to see Jane Lennox yesterday evening to offer our help. She is in an awful state and blaming herself too. She had spent the weekend in Glasgow and intended returning on Sunday evening, but Fenella persuaded her to stay until Monday afternoon. The police notified them. Fenella has returned home with her mother. She feels she's to blame too because she persuaded her mother to spend the weekend away from Syd and the farm. So you see, Ellen, it's no use blaming yourself.

Everyone can't be responsible.'

'Maybe not,' Ellen said doubtfully. 'He must have felt very low though.'

'Apparently he had been very violent towards Jane on Thursday evening when she told him she was going to spend the weekend in Glasgow with Fenella. He struck her several times so she told him if he didn't get help she would leave him altogether because she couldn't go on any longer the way they were. Now she regrets saying that. She called at Doctor Jamieson's surgery on her way to the station and told him he had to persuade Syd to get help because she was at the end of her tether. He gave her something for her bruises and promised to call on Syd at home. Apparently he had done so. His car was there for some time, according to the older man who works at Highfold. Apparently Doctor Jamieson had tried to persuade Syd to go into hospital for treatment but he was adamant he couldn't leave the farm. Eventually he persuaded Syd to take the medication he had brought. We, Sam and I, suspect even the good doctor may be having some regrets because he had not fully understood how badly Syd needed help. Jane says the doctor is adamant that he emphasized Syd must take the medication according to the instructions and he had promised he would. He rarely drank alcohol but when they found him the bottle of pills was empty and he appeared to have drunk quite a lot of whisky.'

'Syd Lennox hasn't been himself since the first time Derek got into trouble with the police,' Sam said firmly. 'It had all got too much for him and I don't think anyone was to blame. He has been neglecting his work for quite a while. All we can do now is help

Jane deal with things.' He looked at Ellen. 'I expect she will want to discuss the tenancy with you once the funeral is past.'

'Of course.' Ellen nodded. 'Will it be a public funeral?'

'No,' Rosemary said. 'They thought it would be better to have it private but Jane is expecting us to go. You too, Alex, as her nearest neighbours, so I'm sure it would be in order for you to accompany Alex as his wife, Ellen. It's not my place to tell you but all Jane wants is to get away from Highfold, to sell everything up as quickly as she can, and leave the area.'

'Oh dear. Poor woman. She must be distraught.'

'She is, but she seemed very sure about that.'

'Is she needing help with the farm?' Alex asked. 'Is there anything I can do?'

'Yes, she needs all the help we can give her.' Sam looked glum. 'I'd say things have been deteriorating for some time. The young worker seems a decent enough lad but he hasn't been there long so he doesn't know much about farming yet. Jane never had much to do with the farm or the book-keeping since Derek left school. She thought Syd didn't want her to know how often he helped Derek out of trouble. She seems utterly bewildered.'

'So who is doing the milking?' Alex asked.

'Billy is home from university for Christmas so he is managing the milking here, with a bit of help from young Toby to do any lifting. I milked the cows at Highfold last night and this morning. Syd Lennox usually did the milking himself so there's nobody else.'

'I'm afraid we shall have nothing but farming for the

rest of the evening now,' Rosemary said, rolling her eyes heavenward. 'But I can understand why Jane wants to sell up as soon as possible. The trouble is it takes ages to arrange a sale, checking ear numbers, printing a catalogue and advertising.'

'It's not a pedigree herd so they could be sold at an ordinary auction, but you're right about the ear tags and I could see at a glance that there's quite a few missing,' Sam declared. 'All the animals will have to be checked and replacement tags ordered and put in their ears before any of them can be moved anywhere. Meanwhile I'm keeping spare wellingtons and overalls in the car to wear when I'm there, in case there's any disease I don't know about yet. As soon as the funeral is over, if you could spare one of your men for a whole day, Alex, we could run all the cattle through the race and make a note of those with missing tags. Fenella is home from university so I expect she will write them down as I call them out. It's better for her to be busy. She should be able to check each number against the registration certificates too. That would be a big help.'

'It would that,' Alex agreed. 'Half the work these days is paperwork. I'll tell you what, though, if Jane Lennox really decides she wants a quick sale, without the trouble of getting the cattle washed and groomed ready for market, I know a dealer over in Wigtownshire who might offer for the whole herd. I know he does that sometimes. She will not get as much money but it would be a lot less bother, especially when she doesn't know much about them and has no reliable men to help her.'

'That would certainly be one solution,' Sam said slowly, 'especially since I shall not be free to help when Billy returns to university, or if milking twice a day, every day, proves too much for him.'

'Oh, Dad!' Billy muttered in exasperation. 'You're still not convinced I can farm, are you?'

'No, I'm not, but you're not the problem right now. Alex, as soon as an opportunity arises I'll mention your suggestion to Jane Lennox. When does the tenancy expire, Ellen?'

'The solicitor stated that we need to know by the end of May,' Ellen said, 'but obviously this changes a lot of things and I would agree to whatever suits her, even if Mrs Lennox wants to leave as soon as she can sell her stock. In fact I'd prefer her to do that, rather than sub-let the farm. That could lead to all sorts of problems. As Kim's trustee I want to do whatever is best.'

The following day Ellen drew Kim aside. 'Highfold Farm will belong to you when you're eighteen, Kim. I'm afraid it will be the bulk of your father's legacy once the taxes have been paid. That makes you almost the landlord. I know you're very young but I think it would be appropriate for you to attend Mr Lennox's funeral with us, if you feel up to it.'

'Aye, I agree,' Alex said. 'You're a sensible lassie and you'll be on holiday from school.'

Billy was surprised to see how upset Fenella was at the funeral considering the trouble and heartache Syd Lennox had caused recently. She had been desperate to get away from home because of him. Kim was standing beside him with Alex on her other side. She watched as the older girl turned to Billy and buried her face against his shoulder. Without hesitation he held her close. It was obvious they knew each other very well. Kim knew it was ridiculous to feel a stab of jealousy at such a time, but it took her unawares.

'I didn't think he would do anything like this,' Fenella sobbed. 'I thought I hated him for the way he treated Mum, and now I feel it's all my fault. I wanted her to spend the weekend with me. I even persuaded her to stay another night. He wouldn't have done it if she'd been there.'

'It's no use blaming yourself, Fen,' Billy said gruffly. 'He must have been terribly depressed. He would have done it another time, or found another way.'

'That's what Doctor Jamieson said, but I can only think of the times when Liam and I were small and he was so patient and kind to us then.'

'If it was anybody's fault I think it was Derek's. It must have been an awful disappointment to his father when he kept getting into serious trouble.'

'Billy's right, lassie,' Alex said, stepping forward. 'And after Derek was killed it's natural for his father to remember only the good things and shut out the way he behaved, just as you're only remembering the good man Syd Lennox used to be. It's as it should be. I hear you're doing well at university and enjoying your course? You will have to concentrate on that now and make your mother proud of you, then you can both put this behind you and move forward.'

'Th–thank you, Mr Caraford,' Fenella said, grateful for Alex's kindly tone and the fact that he didn't blame her for what had happened, but she knew it would be a long time before either she, or her mother, could forgive themselves.

*

Alex had showed Kim how to fill in and check the animal passports against the ear tags which every animal had to have. He was pleased when she showed an interest for he found the increasing record-keeping a laborious job and Kim seemed pleased to help. He mentioned this to Sam and suggested he should ask Kim to help when he went to sort out all the cattle at Highfold. Fenella had not done that sort of thing before but she stood beside the pens where the men were chasing the cattle through and made a note of the numbers for each animal when Sam called them out. She made a separate column for all those who had lost a tag because the regulations demanded they be duplicated. Replacement tags would have to be ordered, purchased and attached before the animals could be moved anywhere.

'I'd no idea all this had to be done,' she said to Sam. 'He – my f–father – never asked for help, not even from Mum.'

'It will be good practice for when you're a qualified vet. You'll have to go round the herds checking for tuberculosis and you need the ear numbers to identify the animals then.'

'Yes, I suppose I shall. It's strange that the government have more regulations for identifying cattle than they do for children, or even adults.'

Sam glanced at her and grinned.

'You don't fancy two big floppy ear tags in your ears, do you? Mind you, implants are beginning to take their place so they can be read off as the animals go by the machine. It will save a lot of time and stress once the snags are ironed out if they can all be done that way.'

Later Fenella went into the house to help Kim sort out the passports. These resembled a cheque book of cards with barcodes and numbers which had already been registered at a central government office. It was essential that the numbers tallied with the numbers on the ear tags.

'I reckon he had a filing system known only to himself,' Fenella muttered as she and Kim struggled to get them into some sort of order.

'I often heard my father grumble when he sold animals through the auction ring and later discovered the farmer had not brought the correct paperwork,' Kim said. 'I didn't understand what he was talking about then.'

'Fenella and I will be truly grateful to Alex Caraford if he can arrange a sale for us with a dealer,' Jane Lennox said, bringing them a cup of coffee. 'A lot of people will think I'm foolish to give up the tenancy immediately but money is not everything. I need peace of mind and I shall never find it here now.' She had forgotten that Kim was a schoolgirl still. She was tall and slim and her young face was serious with concentration.

'I thought Billy might have come to help too,' Fenella said, making no effort to hide her disappointment.

'He is doing the milking at Martinwold while his father is milking the cows here, for your mother. He starts at five in the morning, then he has them all to milk again in the afternoon. Too much standing around is not good for his leg.'

'OK, OK,' Fenella said, quirking an eyebrow. 'I only

asked.' She eyed Kim's increased colour curiously. 'I do believe you're sweet on him.'

'Of course I'm not!' Kim frowned fiercely. 'Anyway, he's my cousin now.'

'Only by marriage. That wouldn't make any difference if you fancied him. He was a lovely guy when he and my brother were friends. Half the girls in my class were sweet on him, including me. Having a peg leg makes a difference though. There will be so many things he can't do. According to Mum, his parents are hoping he will decide on some other kind of career when he finishes university.'

'But he loves the farm, and his animals. He says there are ways round problems if you look for them. I believe he will return home to farm,' Kim protested, 'and I'm sure he will make a success of it.'

'It's not so easy as you think with animals, but we shall see. He's a handsome fellow, isn't he, even if he has lost a leg. I suppose I can't blame you for falling for him, especially when you are so young. I keep forgetting that. You look so much older, especially now you've got a ponytail instead of your plaits.' Kim scowled and got on with the work. She wondered if Fenella was warning her that Billy was hers and she intended to marry him when they both finished at university. She never thought about him having only one leg but she supposed lots of girls would, especially if they were mad about dancing.

Alex was bitterly disappointed with the offer which Lou Hanson, the dealer, made for the Lennox cattle.

'Man, ye canna be serious! I know some of the dairy cows have been a bit neglected recently but at least they are in good condition and most of them are decent commercial cows. Then there's a bunch of good in-calf heifers and another thirty young heifers ready to go to the bull.'

'That's as maybe, but it will be a while before they bring me a profit and there's a lot of dairy farmers going out of business these days. I can pick and choose.'

'Aye and there's a good many herds doubling and trebling numbers, like factory farms. I hear you're supplying a lot of them in your area so don't tell me there's no trade.' The trouble was the dealer had already met Jane Lennox before he looked at her cattle. He knew she was desperate for a quick deal so she could get away from everything. It was like taking sweets from a baby.

'You're taking advantage, man. The woman's come through a lot of trouble. She's still in shock. She'll regret it later if she accepts your offer, and she'll probably blame me then.'

'Take it or leave it. It's all one to me.' Hanson shrugged. Alex sighed heavily. The man was a dealer; they didn't have room for compassion.

'Give her twenty-four hours to decide.'

'I got the impression she'd give me her answer straightaway,' Hanson said huffily. 'I reckon she'll accept it.'

'Maybe she will, but we'll let you know tomorrow,' Alex insisted firmly. In his heart he knew the man was right. When he told Jane the price Hanson was offering, she nodded vaguely. She was younger than him but she looked twenty years older with her pale, strained face.

'I told him we needed until tomorrow to consider,' Alex said. 'He knows you want a quick sale and his offer is barely half their true value. Sleep on it and I'll ask Sam and some of the neighbours if they have any better suggestions. We all owe it to Syd Lennox to get the best prices we can for his herd. That's the last time I shall put any business Hanson's way.'

'You're very kind, but don't worry on our account, Mr Caraford,' Jane said wearily. 'It would give me enough capital to buy a house and get away from here. I'm thinking of taking a year's refresher course in the work I used to do as a hospital technician.'

'I see. Well, I'll call to see you tomorrow in case you change your mind.'

Back at Bengairney, Alex told Ellen he felt let down by the dealer's paltry offer.

'I called in on Sam but he can't think of any other dealer who would take the whole herd off her hands and it's no use somebody picking out the best. They have all to be sold.'

'Surely in the circumstances the local auctioneer could arrange an on-farm sale, even at this short notice?' Ellen suggested. 'Trevor and I managed it more than once for people in trouble, usually bankruptcy, but for whatever reason they needed a quick sale. The machinery will have to be sold anyway and Mr Lennox seemed to have more capital tied up in it than most farmers can afford these days.'

'Yes, he did. We haven't considered that aspect. His son, Derek, always wanted the latest gadgets and Syd Lennox humoured him. He has three good tractors and an old banger for a start, as well as silage machinery and a feeder wagon, the plough, a new seed drill, his Land Rover and cattle trailer and all the small tools and machinery. Aye, now you mention it, Ellen, that will bring a fair amount of money and whatever Jane Lennox thinks now it will all be needed by the time young Fenella gets her education. She may want to buy into a veterinary practice eventually. I'll telephone the auction mart and see if a sale can be arranged at short notice. The trouble is everything closes down for a fortnight over Christmas and New Year. It would be a rush, but Sam can't go on milking cows at Highfold once Billy goes back to university. We would need to aim for a sale by the end of January at the latest. Even if we couldn't get all the cattle clipped and shampooed for the sale day it would be no worse than letting Jane Lennox accept the pittance yon rascal is offering,' he added bitterly.

'You're a good man, Alex,' Ellen said softly. 'There's nothing in all this for you except a lot of hard work preparing.'

'Most neighbours rally round to help if they can in times of trouble. Anyway I reckon I'm the luckiest man on earth these days,' Alex said with a smile and drew her into his arms for a long kiss. They pulled apart when Kim appeared in the kitchen.

'Am I interrupting something?' she asked with a mischievous grin. It made her feel happy and warm inside to see Aunt Ellen with pink cheeks, looking happy and bright eyed.

'Nothing that willna get better with keeping, lassie,' Alex said, returning her smile, his blue eyes crinkling. Kim was pleased he always treated her more as an equal than as an ignorant child. 'I'll give Sam a ring to make sure he agrees and is willing to help, then I'll talk to the auctioneers. Some of the neighbours will lend a hand once they hear we're getting ready for a farm sale, especially knowing Mrs Lennox's circumstances. It's a bit like the five barley loaves and two small fishes in the Bible – brings out the best in folk, well, in some folk anyway.'

Unfortunately the firm of auctioneers said they couldn't squeeze in such a big on-farm sale at short notice, what with Christmas holidays, all the advertising needed, lists and details to be compiled, not to mention sale stickers and purchasers' cards.

'Too many people are on holiday. How would Mrs Lennox like a sale about Easter?'

'I told them Mrs Lennox wouldn't,' Alex muttered when he returned to the kitchen to report. 'Neither could Sam keep on helping all that time. Mrs Lennox would need to employ a relief milker. Some are good, but some are unreliable, even if she can get one.'

'I know it's short notice but I reckon I could do it,' Ellen said, her soft mouth firming with determination. 'I concentrated mainly on the furniture sales once we became established because Trevor didn't know much about antiques and I'd built up that side of our business, but I took a turn at selling with him when we had a big farm sale.'

'But Aunt Ellen, wouldn't you lose your voice if you did it all yourself? And who would do the clerking?' Kim asked. She had listened to these discussions between her father and aunt for as long as she could remember.

Ellen looked at her thoughtfully. 'You're right, Kim.' She frowned in concentration, chewing her lower lip. 'I'll tell you what, though, if we could arrange it for the end of January, my old partner's son, John Price, might come up and lend a hand. He hasn't had time to build up a lot of clients yet. He's young but he has a good voice and a pair of sharp eyes, just like you, Kim. You'll have to stand up beside me and look for any discreet bidders. They are all strangers to me here. You get familiar with the way some people bid with barely a flicker of a muscle, and you get to know what certain customers are likely to want. Yes, I'd like to have a go, Alex, if you're willing? John Price married the clerk out of our offices so he would probably bring Anne with him to lend a hand. They would need to stay with us a couple of nights or so. What do you think?'

'It will depend more what Mrs Lennox decides,' Alex said with a sigh. 'We'll call on her tomorrow morning and see what she's saying, but don't be disappointed if she has decided to let the cattle go for a pittance.'

The following morning Alex had just come in for breakfast after finishing the milking when the telephone rang. Ellen answered it.

'It's Jane Lennox. For you, Alex. She sounds agitated.'

'The man who came to see the cattle, Mr Hanson, telephoned last night,' she said breathlessly. 'He said he needed a quick decision. It was Fenella who answered and she told him our herd was not for sale at the price he was offering. She – she heard your opinion, Mr Caraford, so she told him it needed to be a third higher. He refused and slammed the telephone down. I–I know she's right, and so are you, b–but I don't know what to do now. I know Sam can't keep on helping us out the way he is doing.'

'Don't worry, Mrs Lennox,' Alex said cheerfully. 'We'll come over to see you later this morning. My wife has come up with a suggestion.' He looked up and smiled at Ellen across the kitchen. He liked the words 'my wife'. 'We'll discuss it with you and your daughter and take it from there. Tell Fenella to keep on sorting out those passports though. We can't move anything without them being right.'

'Oh, thank you, thank you so much.' Alex could hear the relief in her voice.

'Thank goodness the girl is tougher than her mother and has seen sense,' Ellen said. 'It can be a harsh world out there. She'll be glad of the money one day.'

Much later, while their elders discussed arrangements for an on-farm sale, Kim helped Fenella sort out and check more of the records.

'Uncle Alex says the new duplicate ear tags will not come until a fortnight after Christmas so we need to keep them separate,' Kim said.

'How come you understand about all this?' Fenella asked curiously. 'I mean, you didn't even live on a farm, did you?'

'Uncle Alex explained all about the ear tags and the birth registrations and he lets me help him when he's tagging the young calves. When I'm helping him in the milking parlour he often tells me about the different cow families and stories about when he and Uncle Sam were boys, and about his parents. Bengairney must have been a very happy place. He remembers some of the grandparents and great-grandparents of cow families which are still in the herd and it makes it all more interesting and easier to remember each one as an individual – rather than just another black and white animal.'

'You really are keen, aren't you?' Fenella mused. 'I used to come out on the farm to help. Ours are not pedigree animals but I loved the calves and we had sheep too, but when Derek left school he was so spiteful and nasty most of the time that I stopped going anywhere near him. I concentrated on my schoolwork, especially once I knew I wanted to be a vet. Liam wasn't interested in farming but he always helped in the holidays because he thought it was our duty to help repay him for giving us a home and food and clothes.'

'Did you always say "him", never Father or Dad?' Kim asked.

'We used to call him Dad, because that's what Derek called him and we couldn't remember our own father. Now that I'm older I think Derek resented us even then. It was only after Derek was killed and he started treating Mother so badly that I stopped calling him Dad. He was always so strong and fit. I didn't understand he was so ill mentally. I hated him latterly but Mum blames herself. She thinks she should have insisted on having him admitted to hospital for his own sake. She was never this pathetic and – and indecisive before.'

'Uncle Alex thinks the shock will wear off. He is very relieved you didn't accept the dealer's offer. He feels responsible and he says she would have blamed him later. They are going to try and organize a sale from the farm. It will be an awful lot of work for everybody. Do you think your mother will cope?'

'It may be good for her. Force her out of her

lethargy, perhaps? Deep down she thinks she has no right to the money from the farm but there are no close relatives and she was his wife for years. She did her best for all of us, including Derek, trying to help him see right from wrong.'

When Billy heard about the farm sale he suggested Michael Appleby might help with compiling the lists of stock and machinery on his computer, drafting adverts about the sale for the local newspapers and printing sale cards. Fenella was secretly pleased by this suggestion but she didn't comment. The more she got to know Michael, the better she liked him, but most of her contact with him was via email rather than in person. She felt instinctively that he was sincere and trustworthy.

'Michael is always pleased to earn some extra cash in the holidays,' Billy said, 'and he has a methodical mind. He's a wiz on the computers.'

Ellen was impressed when he presented some rough proofs to her.

'You can come and clerk for me any day when I begin to have furniture sales,' she told him with a smile.

'Are you really going to set up in business with the furniture? Even now you're married?' Jane Lennox asked.

'Of course. Alex is quite agreeable. I shall keep it small enough to manage – quality more than quantity, but sometimes you need to be able to empty a house completely to pick out the pieces you want. I shall have plenty of storage with the Charmwood barns. I love my work.'

'Do you think you could sell my furniture at the

farm sale? There's only a few things I want to keep. Most of it will not fit in a modern house and I don't want to pay for storage. There were five of us and now there's only me. I don't need all the bedroom suites.'

'You decide what you want to keep then and show me the rest. If you have any antique pieces I will give you a better price than you will get as part of a farm sale, unless you prefer to sell them privately?'

'Oh no. I'd be happy for you to take anything you want.'

'She is grateful, but so naïve I can't believe it,' Ellen said when she and Alex were in bed later that evening. 'She has a beautiful walnut dining table and all the leaves in a stand in the hall. She would have given it to me for the sake of getting it removed. She is delighted with the prices I have offered for that and one of the bedroom suites and a few other smaller items, and I know I can make a profit. There were several valuable ornaments which had belonged to Jane's grandmother. She didn't realize they are valuable until I told her, but she doesn't want to sell them anyway, and I don't blame her.'

The sale was arranged for a Saturday at the end of January so that Billy and Michael could be home to help with the clerking and records and Kim could be present to help Ellen. It was very well attended with neighbours giving their support as buyers and bidders, as well as helping to set out machinery and arrange straw bales for a sale ring. It proved to be a great success and Lou Hanson, the dealer, bought several cows at twice the price he had offered. This amused Alex. Fenella and Jane were both overwhelmed with gratitude.

'I don't know how I could have got through every-thing without your help and organization,' Jane told Ellen, 'and Alex and Sam and Billy have been wonderful. I do believe I shall miss you all now the time has come to leave.'

'Surely you will be back to visit?' Rosemary asked.

'Maybe one day. I am going to stay with my great aunt north of Glasgow for now. I shall look around for a bungalow near to her. She is very frail so she is looking forward to having company. I can't tell you what a relief it will be to feel settled again,' she added with a shudder.

EIGHT

Billy was in his last year at university when his secret misgivings and uncertainties were confirmed, leaving him angry, disillusioned and more wary than ever. He and Michael Appleby were still sharing the same flat where they had started off. They were aware that some of their more lively fellow students considered them a dull pair and referred to them as monks in a joking sort of manner, since neither young man ever boasted of conquests or discussed their private feelings. They were happy with their own circle of friends who shared their tastes in music and films, books and architecture. They worked hard and were reaping academic success from their efforts. Amongst the regular visitors to the flat were three Indian girls, two sisters and their cousin. The girls shared a car and were from a fairly wealthy family. One of them was an excellent musician. She had an electronic organ which went everywhere with her; her cousin played the guitar and so did Michael, although not to the same high standard. When they discovered Billy had a good tenor voice they often enjoyed a musical evening together with plenty of laughter. They trusted each other, knowing their friendship allowed them companionship without commitment.

They accepted that free and easy relationships were commonplace but for Michael his commitment was to his studies and any spare cash was devoted to his personal interests. Billy suspected there was a special girl somewhere in his life but Michael kept his own counsel on the subject and Billy did not pry into other people's affairs. The truth was, Michael was not sure how serious Billy considered his own friendship with Fenella Lennox and he was reluctant to hurt his friend. He had no wish to come between them but on the other hand his own feelings for her were growing into more than friendship. He was afraid Fenella looked upon him in the place of her brother, Liam, as a confidante and friend, and he also feared his family and background might not measure up to Fenella's standards.

Billy never mentioned the reason for his own reticence but he was deeply sensitive about his prosthetic limb and wary about the way many girls might react to the sight of his stump. He needed loyalty and trust before he would consider leaving himself open to ridicule, or worse outright rejection and repulsion. Consequently he never indulged in more than light flirtations.

Usually he and Michael went home together every second weekend so he could do the relief milking and keep in touch with the farm, but Michael was planning to fit in an extra visit as a surprise for his father's fiftieth birthday celebration. His mother had suggested he and his sister might like to invite a friend each. Mary invited Kim since the two remained close friends. It was with some trepidation that Michael eventually invited Fenella to stay for the weekend and meet his family. He didn't know whether he was relieved or discouraged when she said she was unable to get away so yet again he put off mentioning his growing regard for her to Billy.

When some of their fellow students heard that Billy would be spending the weekend alone, they invited him to join them but Billy was working hard and perfectly happy with his own company. He didn't realize that his reserve had become a challenge to some of the girls, or that they considered him handsome and attractive. Pamela Wilson was one such girl. She was popular with both male and female students. She enjoyed life but she was generous with her friendship and often helped girls who were finding it difficult to settle, or boys who were suffering the effects of a broken romance. Billy knew this but he was still surprised when she arrived at his flat that Saturday evening with a DVD and a few bottles of his favourite beer, saying she had come to keep him company because he was on his own for the weekend.

'This beer will last me a week. How did you know it's my favourite?' he asked.

'I asked Michael.'

'I see. Did he know you were coming tonight?'

'Of course not. It was a spur of the moment thing when I realized we would both be alone. Ben has gone home this weekend as well.'

'Ben?'

'Dear me, Billy, you never keep up, do you?' She

chuckled. 'Ben Jardine is my current beau.'

'I'd have a struggle to keep up with the rate you girls chop and change your partners.'

The living room of the flat had one easy chair and a small settee. Billy usually claimed the settee so that he could rest his leg more easily and when he and Michael were alone he sometimes removed his artificial limb and hopped his way to bed later. He was glad he had not removed it before Pam arrived. Almost as soon as the film (a scary one) began, she moved to sit beside him. It was not long before she snuggled closer, reminding him of the way Kim used to do, except Kim had had a childish innocence. He smiled at the thought. She was seventeen now and her cuddles were no longer spontaneous. In fact, he had noticed a new reserve. She was not so natural and at ease with him as she used to be and she didn't drop into the milking parlour and offer to help him as often either. He missed both her help and her humour because she often made him laugh with her dry retorts and quirky idea of fun. It was Michael who told him Kim and Mary were both learning to drive.

'You didn't hear a word I said,' Pamela remarked, poking him gently in the ribs. She was beginning to realize she would have to use all her feminine attractions because she had no intention of failing. 'You were miles away.'

'Oh, was I? Sorry. What did you say?' he asked, jerking his attention away from thoughts of Kim. As Mary's closest friend she was going to be at the Applebys' family party tonight. 'I suppose I'm a bit tired, that's all,' he added apologetically. 'We're usually in bed by midnight and it's nearly one o'clock.'

'So it is. I was asking if I could make both of us a drink of hot chocolate? You go and get ready for bed and I'll bring yours in for you before I leave. Don't worry, I'll make sure the latch is down so the door is locked when I go,' she added quickly when he frowned and hesitated. It seemed the easiest and quickest way to end the evening, Billy thought, and wondered later how he could have been so naïve. Pam certainly took plenty of time and he was almost asleep by the time she pushed open the bedroom door and appeared with two mugs of steaming hot chocolate. He gasped. She was wearing an almost transparent black negligée which left little to the imagination. She handed him a mug then perched close beside him on the bed. Later Billy couldn't believe he had allowed himself to be so easily seduced but he didn't try to pretend to himself that he didn't enjoy the experience and he knew Pam had too. He was a healthy and virile young man and he would have had to be blind not to know he was attractive.

Although it was not an evening he intended to repeat, he was thoroughly deflated when he overheard one of the girls talking with a group of friends a few days later. Michael was with him and the way he tried to draw him away made him realize his flatmate already knew what they were discussing and had probably heard it already.

'She only did it because two of us had a bet with her that she couldn't get him into bed and find out what it was like with a cripple. We didn't think she would want to do it really, or that she could. I mean, he's usually such a monk. Ben was furious with her when he heard why she had done it, especially when she said he might be a peg-leg but he was just as good as him in bed, if not better.'

'So, it didn't make any difference then, him having only one leg, I mean?' one of the other girls asked curiously. Michael tried again to draw him away but Billy's face was set, and very pale. He shrugged him off.

'Pam says it made her shudder at the thought of seeing some kind of stump on the bed so she never looked at it, but it can't have made that much difference if he was as good as she says. Ben has finished with her because of the bet, but she got the money. She insisted we had to pay up because she bought a DVD and some beer as an excuse to get in. It cost us a fiver each.' Billy winced and obeyed Michael's tug on his sleeve. It was not a subject either of them ever mentioned again but Billy knew he would not forget.

Michael was relieved when the prospect of a trip abroad pulled Billy out of his grim mood. One of the lecturers was arranging a trip to Holland to see some dairy robots with demonstrations of the cows being milked.

'We shall be away four days. Apart from the travelling, two of the days will be hectic and very tiring with a lot of walking and standing. There will not be much rest. Are you sure you're up to it?' his lecturer asked. Billy insisted that he was and it was the sort of thing he needed to see in operation.

'I'm determined to go, whatever it does to my bloody leg,' he said to Michael. 'Even if they end up cutting off the rest of it.'

'Hey, don't talk like that. Nothing's worth that happening,' Michael said in alarm.

'I might never get the chance to visit the factory again, and they're taking us to farms to see the robots working. I believe these things are the future for dairy farmers. How much longer do you think men will want to milk cows seven days a week and start at five o' clock every morning?'

'I don't know much about it. I suppose dairy farming is very labour intensive,' Michael agreed, 'but these machines will still need someone to operate them, won't they?'

'You're as bad as my father,' Billy said, giving Michael a playful punch. 'They need someone to oversee them and make sure they're working properly but it's not a set routine like milking a herd of cows twice a day in a milking parlour. If what I've read is true the robot telephones you if there is a problem, even if it's during the night.'

'A robot telephones you? Ach, tell that to the marines!' Michael threw back his head and laughed. 'I don't believe that!'

'Well, I'll tell you whether it's true when I've seen them. The trouble is this is the only time the firm could fit us in because there's a group of farmers going as well, but it's just a fortnight before my final exams.'

'I'm sure you don't need to worry about that. You've sailed through everything so far, as well as doing those courses with computers. Is it true that you can get tractors with a computer which can plough without a driver?'

'At a price,' Billy agreed. 'Everything will be run

with computers, or satellites, before long. We shall need people to understand them though.'

Kim never derided Billy's suggestion that robots for milking would be commonplace before long. She knew Billy read widely, especially about any ideas which might help him make a success as a farmer and make his disability less of a burden. She knew now that there were some tasks he would never be able to do and her young heart ached for him.

When it came to deciding her own career, she refused to go away to university or to a residential college.

'I feel more settled and happy at Bengairney than I have ever been in my life so far,' she said. 'I don't want to leave home now.' Ellen could understand how she felt and Alex was pleased she found his old home such a happy place to live.

'My mother would have been pleased to hear you say that, Kim,' he said. 'She always made Bengairney a happy, welcoming place, but your aunt and I both think you should continue your studies. What about the new local university?'

'I suppose I could make enquiries about the courses,' Kim said doubtfully. 'I wouldn't mind getting some qualifications so long as I could still live here and come home every night.'

'I'm sure you'll soon pass your driving test now you're seventeen. We'll buy you a car, lassie,' Alex said, 'then you would be able to drive yourself in each day.' So she had decided on a course in business studies for which she could choose different modules, with emphasis on accounts and taxation.

'They're subjects which affect all businesses, including farming and auction sale rooms,' she said, 'and I want to stay here and help both of you if I can.'

She was also studying labour law and public liability and she planned to do a more advanced course on computers the following year.

'Nearly everything involves computers,' she said. 'I've done pretty well with them at school so that should make it a bit easier. I'm happier now than I ever believed I could be when Daddy died,' she added.

'I'm pleased to hear you say that, lassie and you know we love having you around,' Alex said. 'We're not pushing you away, but we want to give you every opportunity to make your way in life, and be able to earn a living.'

'But I really do want to stay here and help both of you. You both have book-keeping and accounts to do.'

'That's true enough,' Ellen conceded, 'and I would miss your help with the business already, now that I've built up some stock and I'm acquiring a private clientele. Mrs Brex is useful for dusting around and keeping an eye on things if I have to go out to a sale, or see a client, but she has no idea how to deal with customers who drop in unexpectedly. Her feathers get as ruffled as a broody hen. She doesn't seem to realize it is my business to welcome customers if I'm to sell to them. It was a good idea of yours to set up the website, Kim, and show off our wares, but I don't think I could manage that myself.'

'Good!' Kim grinned. 'So if you need me that means you agree I can stay at home and travel to college each day, and then work for both of you when I've finished the course?'

'I guess so, but don't blame us if you think you've missed out on the fun of student days,' Ellen warned. Later on when she and Alex were alone she said, 'I think I know the real reason Kim doesn't want to go away from home.'

'Why is that? She's always been sensible and mature for her age and she's done exceptionally well at school according to the guidance teacher,' Alex said. 'I can't believe she would be homesick, especially if we get her a car so she can come home whenever she wants.' He shrugged. 'I'd miss her lively presence about the house, mind you, but I want whatever makes her happy.'

'You're a good man, Alex,' Ellen said warmly. 'I've been so lucky. But I don't think it's us Kim minds leaving. I think she's hero-worshipped Billy for a long time now, almost since we arrived up here, in fact, but she's grown up a lot this past eighteen months. I think her feelings are getting more serious. Billy will be finished at university and coming home in another month. I think she doesn't want to be away when he's living here again.'

'They've always got on well together, the pair of them,' Alex mused, frowning thoughtfully. 'But she's far too young to be serious about anybody yet. You don't think Billy has been encouraging her, do you?' he asked sharply. 'If he has I'll be having a word with that young fellow. I don't want him hurting our lassie.'

Ellen smiled and moved to hug him.

'We're both lucky,' she said, 'Kim as well as me. You're very protective with her. In fact I think you would spoil her if she was the type to be spoiled.

In this instance I don't think you can blame Billy. I doubt if he has even noticed she is no longer a schoolgirl. Boys take longer to grow up and mature than girls. Besides, underneath his handsome and confident façade I have a feeling that Billy could be easily hurt himself. He's more sensitive than he wants us to believe. Losing a leg must be a terrible blow to a fit young man who had enjoyed sport and who has run around the farm since he could toddle.'

'Aye, it must have been a big blow to him, but he's never made a fuss. It was a blow to all of us. Sam and Rosie still worry and wonder if they're doing the right thing letting him come home to farm.'

'His heart is in it and his mind is made up. I think he'll make a success. He may want to make changes to suit his own abilities, but who could blame him for that?'

'You have a soft spot for Billy yourself, I think?' Alex looked curiously at his wife's serious face. 'Are you telling me you wouldn't mind if my nephew and your niece were to become a couple?'

'Only if it is what they both want and if they can make each other happy,' Ellen said seriously. 'I never believe in interfering in other people's lives, certainly not when it comes to something as serious as marriage. Anyway they're both too young for serious commitments. Anything can happen in the next few years. I hear Fenella Lennox is coming to work as a student for the summer in our local veterinary practice. I always thought Billy had feelings for her, but only time will tell.'

'I wonder where she's staying. I didn't think the Lennoxes would want to come back.'

'I heard she will be staying with the family of her old schoolfriend, according to Mrs Brex, and she usually knows all the gossip.'

NINE

Ellen's intuition regarding Kim's youthful yearnings was near the mark. She had really looked forward to Billy coming home for good from university but almost the first time she visited Martinwold after he had settled into a work routine she walked round to the building where the young calves were housed and heard him and Fenella laughing together. True, one of the older vets was there too, but he was busy injecting one of the calves. Kim saw Billy clap Fenella on the back then give her an affectionate hug. She didn't wait for more but turned away and drove home in the little yellow car she had intended to show to Billy.

Once or twice she called at Martinwold in the evening to ask if Billy would like to go swimming with her and Mary but he never seemed to be there.

'He's gone to meet Fenella and some of their old schoolfriends at Gino's,' Rosemary said one night. 'He's never been back there since the night of the accident but Fenella persuaded him to go while she's here. I'm pleased he agreed. It's time he laid old ghosts to rest and got on with his life. You should join them, dear. It's where all the young folk meet. Mary and her brother will probably be there too.'

'No, they're not. Michael has started his new job so he was moving to Glasgow this week. Mary is home from university so I'm collecting her to go swimming. We just thought Billy might like to come too but it doesn't matter.' She gave what she hoped was a nonchalant shrug but Rosemary eyed her shrewdly as she made her way back to her little car. She thought Kim looked unusually despondent, and wondered if Ellen and Alex were working her too hard while she was on holiday from college. She didn't know that Kim insisted on working. She enjoyed helping with both the farm and the antiques. She enjoyed history and learning about the background to various objects, especially furniture of different periods. She often enjoyed looking through Ellen's reference books and she was already quite knowledgeable with information she had subconsciously absorbed from her aunt. She made up her mind she must not pester Billy so it was better to keep busy. She remembered Fenella telling her she had had a crush on him when they were at school; she had wondered then if Fenella was warning her off. Mary seemed to think Michael also had a girlfriend but he was keeping her identity a secret.

The summer Kim had so looked forward to was almost over and she was glad. Fenella Lennox had finished working with the local vets and gone back north to stay in her flat, although university was not due to start for another fortnight.

'I wondered if she was hoping our local vets would take her on in the practice when she finishes next year,' Alex said, 'but I reckon she would be better cutting her teeth with strangers in another area before she settles down where folks know her.'

'Cutting her teeth?' Ellen asked with a frown.

'Learning the practical side. Making her mistakes somewhere else until she's used to the real down-to-earth world of veterinary practice. Most young vets have a lot to learn when they first leave university and most of them make mistakes so it would be better if she made them amongst strangers, especially if she does mean to settle down here permanently.'

'You think she will? Return to live round here, I mean?'

'I don't know. She spent a lot of time with Billy while she was here and they've known each other a long time.'

'I see.' Ellen glanced across at Kim but she was pretending to be absorbed in the book she was studying.

It was late November and the weather forecast had warned there would be snow showers in several areas but few people were prepared for the blizzard which started around midday and kept on coming. Alex had travelled down the M6 to a farm sale early that morning. Ellen had planned to spend the whole day at Charmwood Antiques. Most customers seemed to enjoy wandering from room to room to see pieces in appropriate settings but she wanted to complete a comprehensive inventory and price some of the smaller items she had acquired recently. When the snow began to fall thick and fast she was aware of Mrs Brex glancing out of the windows every few minutes to view the long drive to the main road. Her fidgety manner distracted Ellen and she sighed.

'I expect it will have cleared by nightfall,' she said with a sigh, 'but there will be no customers today so you would be better to go home now, Mrs B.' The woman obeyed with an alacrity which made Ellen smile. Although the snow was not falling so heavily as the November day began to darken, the wind had risen, driving it into hedges and making drifts and ridges, filling roadside ditches and generally obliterating the usual road signs and landmarks. The telephone shrilled, disturbing the silence of the large house. Ellen lifted the receiver with a sigh, stretching her aching back as she did so. Time to call a halt today, she thought.

'Mrs Caraford, this is Mr Forden from the Lodge at your road end.'

'Ah, hello, Mr Forden. Is your wife not so well again?'

'She's fine, thank you. That's not why I'm phoning this time,' he added with a smile in his voice. Ellen had chauffeured his wife to hospital more than once when she had taken one of her turns. 'I thought I should warn you if you're still up at your showrooms. There's a tree down across the drive. It's the big beech tree just after the bend. I didn't want you to come on it suddenly and crash.'

'Gosh! It's such a huge tree. I can't believe it....'

'It's true. I got a shock too. I was taking the wee dog for a last walk before dark when we came on it. It will take most of a day to clear it. Will you be all right up there? Have you food and will you be warm enough? You're welcome to stay at the Lodge with us for the night but you would have to walk down the drive and through the bushes.'

'That's very kind of you, Mr Forden, but I shall be all right up here. I usually have my lunch here so I always keep a small stock of food. The house is warm too so if you don't mind I shall stay safe and warm where I am. I do thank you for letting me know about the tree, though.'

Ellen put the phone down and looked at her watch. Kim would have left the college and be heading home now so she would give her time to get in before she phoned Bengairney. She frowned, wondering if Alex was on his way back up the M6 yet and if the snow was as bad down there. It didn't worry her spending the night on her own but she was thankful she had taken Alex's advice and kept the kitchen for their private use with its Aga. She always had milk and bread, a few tins of soup, cheese and fruit. She wouldn't starve. She smiled to herself. She had a choice of beds, not to mention three chaise longue and a couple of settees. The smile turned to a frown as a sudden gale whistled round the house, rattling the windows. She always kept a couple of travelling rugs in the car, usually for wrapping around pieces of furniture, but she might be glad of them if the storm put the electricity off. She would get the torch too. She had no candles here but then she'd never expected to be spending the night here. She had the beautiful antique oil lamp but that wouldn't be much use without paraffin. She grabbed her anorak and zipped herself up. Even the short distance to the car left her cold and breathless. The phone was ringing again when she opened the door. She was tempted to ignore it but she dumped her stuff in the hall and ran to lift the receiver.

'Oh, Aunt Ellen, thank goodness you're still there. I tried the farm but....'

'Kim? Kim, are you all right?' Ellen knew she wasn't. Her niece had learned at an early age to control her emotions but her voice was shaking. 'Where are you?'

'Stuck in a ditch.' She gave a tremulous laugh, and tried to reassure her aunt. 'I'm all right but the car behind skidded into me and knocked me into what seems to be a ditch at the side of the road. He – he's bashed the back of my car.'

'Never mind that. It will mend, so long as you're all right. But I'm wondering what to do, who to get to pull you out. Alex won't be back for ages and I can't get out because there's a tree blocking the bottom of the drive. I'll phone Sam and see if he can recommend a breakdown lorry. Are you warm enough, Kim?'

'Yes, I'll be fine, so long as I don't have to stay here all night. The man who knocked me into the ditch doesn't seem to be able to shift his car either. He keeps revving furiously.'

'Stay in your car and keep it locked. I'll let you know what's happening, dear.'

It was Rosemary who answered the telephone at Martinwold and Ellen explained their predicament.

'I'll go and tell Sam. He'll probably take the Land Rover and tow Kim's car out of the ditch. Don't worry, Ellen. We'll make sure Kim is all right and we'll keep you informed.'

Sam and Billy were in the cubicle shed, gathering the cows up ready for the milking parlour. Sam immediately said he would go to the rescue.

'I'll come with you, Dad,' Billy said. 'Toby can start the milking until we get back.'

'There's no need for you to come,' Sam said. 'You're safer here. The roads are bad.'

'Oh, for goodness' sake, Dad,' Billy said angrily, 'when will you start treating me like a normal man? You might need me to tie the rope to pull Kim's car out, or to guide you. Anyway she might be hurt or suffering from shock and we need to get her car back home.'

'Well, you'll not be able to drive it. It's not an automatic and you're not insured.'

'I'm coming anyway,' Billy insisted stubbornly. Rosemary and Sam raised their eyebrows and looked at each other. Sam shrugged.

'We'd better get the towing bar as well as a rope then in case we have to tow the car home.'

When they found Kim's yellow car, the darkness made things more difficult but it was evident they needed to pull the car out from behind Kim's before they could do anything else.

'Have you exchanged names and addresses and insurances?' Sam asked.

'Yes, and I've made a note of his registration number,' Kim said. The young man had been reluctant to give her any details. He knew he had been driving too fast and too close behind considering it was a minor road and conditions were bad, and he already had points on his licence.

'I brought the blue flasher and one of the flashing lights off the tractor,' Billy said, as two more cars drew up. 'It will help warn the other cars as they approach.'

'We'll wait while you pull him out,' the first driver offered. 'It will be safer and give you more room to manoeuvre.'

'Thanks,' Sam said. 'That's a great help and better for everybody if we can clear the road.' Billy tied the rope to the rear of the man's car then guided his father in the Land Rover as he carefully pulled the car far enough back onto the road for the driver to straighten up. It was not too difficult and Billy went to untie the rope. He had barely loosened the knot before the young man shot away, sending a flurry of snow into Billy's face and forcing him to jump aside. In his haste Billy slipped and fell backwards. He uttered a curse but before he could move Kim was out of her car and crouching beside him, seething with angry indignation at the man's behaviour.

'Billy, for God's sake, are you all right, son?' Sam asked, rushing to his side.

'I'm fine. I'm all right,' Billy snapped, exasperated with himself for falling over. Before he could try to rise, Kim and his father had hauled him onto his feet. He had forgotten how strong Kim was these days in spite of her slender build. She had once told him she got her muscles from helping Aunt Ellen move her furniture around. The driver of the first waiting car joined them in spite of the snow wetting his shoes and trouser bottoms.

'There's gratitude for you!' he said angrily. 'Did that bastard even say thank you?'

'No, he didn't, and Billy could have been seriously hurt,' Kim said. The lights from the Land Rover showed the twin flags of indignant colour staining her cheeks. 'But I've got his address and I shall let him know what I think of him.'

'Now there's a champion for you,' the man said in a low voice to Billy. He winked. 'I'd say it was almost worth a tumble in the snow.' He turned to Kim. 'If you have his registration number, I'll mention it to a friend of mine in the police force. Young men like that need to learn some road sense, as well as some consideration. I take it he ran into the back of you and pushed your car into the ditch?'

'Yes, he did. He tried to pass and skidded into me, then he tried to deny it was his fault.'

'Right,' Sam said, tying the rope in place himself, 'you jump in, lassie, and stay safe. I shouldn't think there's any damage to the steering but you never know and the far light may be broken.'

'My poor wee car,' Kim sighed as she climbed in.

'I'll get in beside you when we get you on the road,' Billy said, noting she was trembling with reaction and trying not to show it. Apart from a large dent in the back of the car and a twisted front bumper, Kim's car was fit to drive.

'You go in front, lassie, and we'll drive behind in the Land Rover,' Sam said. 'Go slowly. It will be better when we get to the main road. The gritting lorries will probably have been out now.'

'Aye, I think this has taken everybody by surprise,' the driver of the waiting car said. 'It didn't look like snow this morning when I left home. '

'I suppose it's the time of year,' Sam said, 'but so long as no one is injured.'

'I'll travel with Kim in case she's nervous, Dad,' Billy told his father. 'Do you mind if I stay with her at Bengairney until Uncle Alex gets home? Ellen is stuck up at the antiques centre for the night.'

'All right. But he'll not be able to drive your car for you, Kim. You understand that? He has no licence or insurance to cover a manual gearbox.'

'I know,' Kim nodded. 'But it would be good to have company. I know it's silly now that everything is all right but I can't stop shaking.'

'It's reaction,' the other driver said, his mouth tight. 'I'll see the police know about that arrogant young sod, never fear.'

'You'll be fine when we get going,' Sam said, knowing there was no alternative. 'Billy, you realize Alex could be very late by the time he gets over Shap. It's usually worse there than here.'

'I know. We'll keep you posted if he phones. If he's too late or too tired to drive me home I may stay the night. It's Saturday so Kim could drive me home in his Land Rover in time for the milking in the morning. What d'you think?'

'So long as you let us know before we go to bed. You know how your mother worries.'

'OK, will do,' Billy nodded. 'You both worry too much,' he muttered in an undertone as he climbed in beside Kim.

'They worry because they love you, Billy. You should be grateful that they care. I doubt if my mother ever did, or would have done even if she had lived.'

'It can be a bit irritating when people keep reminding me I'm not normal,' Billy said. 'Do you feel bitter about your mother, Kim?' He had never heard her mentioned before.

'Not bitter, no. I never knew her. Anyway Daddy and Aunt Ellen made up for her absence. They took me to all sorts of places children wouldn't normally be allowed to go. I think that's why I always felt more grown up than most of my schoolfriends. Mary is sensible and mature because of her upbringing. I think that's why we get on so well. I've been so lucky. Uncle Alex is a lovely man.' She smiled in the darkness. 'He's as protective as if he'd been my own father.'

In spite of his determination to be a normal man, Billy was wary of the slippery yard. He didn't want to make a fool of himself by falling again so he was glad when Kim drove close to the door at Bengairney.

'No good both of us getting wet feet,' she said cheerfully. 'Here's the key. Will you put the kettle on? I'm dying for a hot drink and you'll need to wait while I cook our evening meal because Aunt Ellen isn't home.'

'Right you are, boss.' Billy grinned, and gave a mock salute. Kim grinned back at him and felt her spirits rise. They were back to their old teasing and camaraderie, like they used to be before she began to feel the little darts of jealousy which had accompanied the pangs of growing up and being aware that Billy was a man and as attractive to other women as he was to her. At least for this evening she would have him to herself. She knew some of the girls from college would know how to make the most of such an opportunity and they considered her old-fashioned and prim. Maybe she was. She drove her battered little car into the shed and locked the doors.

The Carafords had been at Bengairney for fifty years and Billy was familiar with the layout of the house because he had stayed there often when his granny and grandfather had been alive, but the kitchen had been restyled since Ellen moved in.

'My, this is posh,' he greeted Kim when she joined him. 'I've put the kettle on the hotplate. Is that right?'

'Yes, that's it singing already. The Aga gets hot when

the lids have been down all day. Do you fancy tea or coffee, or something else? Supper will be a while – do you want a scone or some of the chocolate cake I made? It's a new recipe and Uncle Alex says it's as good as his mother used to make.'

'That's a rare compliment then. My granny was well known for her cooking. Mum uses a lot of her recipes. Do you like cooking, Kim?'

'Yes, I like experimenting. Aunt Ellen has certain recipes which she does extremely well but she doesn't like trying out new ideas so she lets me cook whenever I have time.'

'In that case I'd better have a scone and the chocolate cake in case you're intending to experiment on me tonight.'

'That's good. If I get a casserole in soon it will be easy to warm up when Uncle Alex gets in. Aunt Ellen said on the phone that he has no idea when he will get home. It depends what the motorway is like when he eventually gets back to it. I think the farm sale was quite a distance away on country roads.'

'Mmm, this is delicious,' Billy said as he licked the chocolate fudge icing from his forefinger. 'You can come and experiment on me any time, Miss Kimberley Wilshaw.'

'Will you put a match to the fire in the wee television room, please, Billy, while I get on with chopping up the meat and vegetables?' Kim asked, briskly clearing away the remains of their snack. 'The heating will be coming on about now but the fire makes it cosy on a night like this.'

'Did you get central heating put in when Uncle Alex married? It used to be electric storage heaters and coal fires in Gran's time. Mum and Dad tried to persuade Uncle Alex to get oil heating after Granny died but he said he couldn't face the upheaval.'

'He said he hadn't done anything to the house but now that he owns it he said Aunt Ellen could make whatever alterations she liked so long as she didn't bankrupt him and he didn't have to clean up the mess. She and Daddy were both quite thrifty but she has redecorated most of the rooms since the heating and the double-glazed windows were installed.'

'That must be a great improvement.'

'Yes, it is. Aunt Ellen is thinking of inviting your family and your Aunt Tania's for Christmas here now that everything is tidy again. I used to love Christmas when Daddy was alive.' She gave a wistful sigh.

'I'm sure it will be good again, if we can all be together as a family, Kim,' Billy said comfortingly. 'Of course you'll need to get some mistletoe,' he teased.

'I shouldn't think your Ritchie cousins need the mistletoe to steal kisses from what I've seen of them?' Kim said, quirking an eyebrow.

'No, you're right there. I wish I had half their confidence. Of course they have plenty of money so I don't suppose any of the girls reject them anyway.'

'Oh Billy, I'm sure it takes more than money to attract nice girls.'

'Yes, it takes a man with two good legs,' Billy said. Kim's eyes widened at the note of bitterness. She had never heard him sound so down before. She wondered if Fenella Lennox had rebuffed his advances after spending so much time together during the summer.

Two hours later, Kim was about to serve up their meal when the telephone rang.

'It's Uncle Alex,' she said, covering the mouthpiece. 'He hasn't got as far as Shap yet and he's stopped for something to eat so it's going to be very late before he gets home. He sounds worried. He's pleased I have company but he wants to speak to you.'

Kim could only hear Billy's side of the conversation but she saw his mouth tighten and heard his responses getting more terse.

'For God's sake, Uncle Alex, don't you trust me? Would you rather I left her on her own?' He listened, then broke in, 'I have too much respect for her to take advantage,' and put the telephone down.

'Can we eat now?' Kim asked, realizing that Billy was upset and angry over something his uncle had said.

'Yes. I mean, yes, please, let's do that. I didn't mean to snap at you, Kim. I'll telephone my father later and tell him I shall not be home until morning. Uncle Alex says his herdsman will look round the cows here tonight so we have not to go out.' His mouth tightened again. 'He's afraid I might fall and then I'd be a burden to you trying to get me to my feet. I'm not that stupid! Anyway, I'm not that helpless either, even if it does take me a bit longer than a normal fellow to get up.'

'Forget about everyone else. Come and enjoy your meal. Uncle Alex says he will not want anything except a hot drink and I've to leave the kettle on. So you can eat as much as you like, but I have made you a pudding with meringues, fruit and cream.'

'Thank you, Kim,' Billy said warmly. 'Now you mention it I'm famished and that smells wonderful. What is it?'

'It's pork casserole with carrots, onions and parsnips and a few herbs. I've made creamed potatoes separately and there's peas and apple sauce too if you want it. I love plenty of vegetables.'

Kim was pleased when he accepted a second helping.

'That was delicious,' Billy said as he scraped up the last of his meringue. 'Now I'd better phone Dad as I promised to let him know what's happening with Uncle Alex.' He fished his mobile out of his pocket.

'All right, you phone while I load the dishwasher then I'll make some coffee and bring it through to the room. Would you put some logs on the fire first, please?'

'OK. Sometimes I think you're about the only person who treats me as half normal,' Billy said with a wry grimace.

'Of course I'm not. You can phone in the room if you like. We get quite good mobile reception in there.'

When Kim entered the room carrying the tray of coffee and homemade biscuits, Billy was still talking to his father.

'For God's sake, Dad, not you too! Yes, Uncle Alex said much the same sort of thing.' Kim put the tray down and crept out again, unwilling to eavesdrop on a private conversation but she couldn't help overhearing his voice raised in anger.

'I know she's young and attractive and possibly innocent too but I'm not that desperate that I need to …' He listened. His voice lowered and Kim didn't hear what he said but moments later he called to her.

'Ready for the coffee now?' she asked brightly.

'Yes, please.' He sighed. 'Do you trust me, Kim?'

'Trust you?' Kim stared at him, holding a half-filled cup of coffee.

'Yes, trust me to spend the night here, alone with you, I mean?' His tone was bitter. 'It seems both my own father and my precious uncle think I might take advantage of your innocence or molest you, or some other bloody thing. Don't they realize if you had gone away to university you might have been sharing a flat with men or women every night, for God's sake?'

'Here, drink your coffee,' Kim said flatly, eyeing him warily, 'and if you mean can I trust you with my reputation, then of course I do.' Sometimes I wish I didn't, she thought miserably. Billy never made the sort of advances towards her which other boys did – and some of them she detested, then they taunted her about being unnatural.

'They must think I'm so desperate I need to push my attentions on you the minute the opportunity arises,' he muttered angrily. 'I can think of a few girls when I might have been tempted to take advantage of the situation, but I respect you too much for anything like that, Kim. I hope you know that?'

'Oh yes, I know that,' Kim muttered into her coffee cup. Billy frowned. She turned on the television but neither of them could settle to watch. Billy sensed something he had said had upset Kim but he didn't know what. After the day's work and the freezing cold outside, the big meal and the warmth of the fire, he couldn't stifle a yawn. When he excused himself a second time, Kim said abruptly, 'I can see you're tired.' Or bored, she thought miserably. 'I'll make up the bed in your father's old room. We may as well get an early night. There will be plenty of snow to clear in the morning and Uncle Alex and I will need to rescue Aunt Ellen.'

Billy didn't argue. Their earlier camaraderie seemed to have disappeared like smoke up the chimney, leaving only tension between them. He was still angry with his father and uncle. Was it so obvious that he admired Kim? He knew she was too young for him to consider seriously. Surely they should have realized he respected her too much to take advantage just because they were spending the night alone together? Maybe he should start taking out other girls again to throw them off the scent. He had spent plenty of time with Fenella Lennox during the summer but that was different; they enjoyed each other's company and they could discuss the past and Liam, something neither of them could do with anyone else. Both knew there were no strings attached to their friendship. In fact, Billy was beginning to suspect Fenella and Michael Appleby were in closer contact than he had realized.

TEN

The snow had disappeared by Christmas and heavy rain had washed away any lingering drifts beneath the hedges and behind the stone walls. Only Criffel and a few other high peaks still wore white caps. The weather made little difference to the festive spirits at Bengairney as the family gathered together in the warm and cheery house. Kim had decorated the Christmas tree and retrieved the various decorations she had known since childhood. She had even hung the mistletoe in the hall. Ellen glowed with happiness as Alex praised her cooking.

'I can't take all the credit,' she said, smiling. 'Kim made the starter and the puddings.'

'I'm lucky to be blessed with two talented women,' Alex said. He looked across at Tania's son, Steve. 'You make sure you get a wife who can cook and look after you, laddie. All that glamour I hear you chasing after....' He shook his head. 'Ach, that's no use on its own.' Steve flushed a little. He enjoyed being seen with glamorous girls.

'I've plenty of time to choose if I wait as long as you,

Uncle Alex,' Steve retorted.

'There's no need for that sort of remark,' his father rebuked and Tania gave a repressive frown, not that it ever did any good with Steve.

'I don't know where Steve has sprung from,' she said. 'I don't remember you and Sam being like that when we were young, Alex? He doesn't take his flirting from Struan or me, and I'm sure none of his grandparents were like that.'

'Don't worry,' Alex said. 'He'll learn one day.' He glanced at Ellen and smiled. 'My prize was well worth waiting for, but it's time we made up for waiting so long. I'm planning to take things easier and have more holidays together now that Kim is growing up and doesn't need us, but so far our plans never seem to work out.'

'I know the feeling,' Sam said with a sigh. 'You'll never have time for holidays while you have a dairy herd. Now that we have Billy back home we're going to have a holiday in the spring. Isn't that right, sweetheart?' He winked at Rosemary. He could still make her blush even though they were a long-married couple.

'I'll believe it when I'm there, in some exotic place or other,' she said with a grin.

'Ah, then you haven't seen the brochures I brought from the travel agent? I left them on the kitchen table.'

'Oh, I did see them, but they were all for cruises.'

'Yes, I thought we might try a short cruise to start with and see how we like it. Ten days in May, I thought, before we start the silage. All the cattle will be out to grass by then. Why don't you and Ellen come with us, Alex?' Sam asked. He liked his new sister-in-law and he knew

Rosemary and Ellen had renewed their early friendship.

'We–ell, it's an idea. What do you think, Ellen?'

'Sounds good to me. Kim will still be at college but I could close down the antiques centre for a week and Mrs Brex will keep an eye on things and take any messages. Mmm, I think we would enjoy it with the four of us.'

'What about you and Struan, Tania?' Rosie asked. She had been friends with Sam's sister since they were children.

'I'm sure we'd love to come but we have promised to visit Struan's sister in Australia this spring and we couldn't possibly go all that way and not stay with Carol too.'

'Oh, lucky you!' Rosemary said wistfully, thinking of her beloved daughter on the other side of the world. 'I know she'd love to have you. I suspect she still gets homesick. We can talk to her on Skype now but it's still not the same as being there. Angus is growing so fast too. He'll be past wanting cuddles from his granny by the time we see him.'

'If Billy manages all right while we're away on a cruise we'll go to visit her ourselves later in the year,' Sam promised. He missed his daughter too. 'How about next Christmas?'

'We shall have to wait and see how Billy gets on first,' Rosemary said doubtfully.

'Oh, Mother! I shall manage everything fine,' Billy said with a note of irritation. 'And I should get on even better if I could persuade you and Dad to let me install a couple of robots.'

'If we did that we'd have no money left to go to

Australia,' Sam said lightly.

'I'm serious, Dad. And there's ways round the capital outlay if that's really the problem. It is the way dairy farmers will go in the future.'

'This discussion is not for the Christmas dinner table,' Rosemary said firmly. She had heard the argument over robots between Billy and Sam several times recently and she knew it could go on a long time and could become heated.

'I don't know anything about robots,' Steve chipped in, serious for once, 'but Cousin Billy is right about the herds expanding, isn't he, Dad?'

'Yes,' Struan acknowledged, 'but I don't know much about robots, or whether they're worth the capital outlay.'

'You'll know better than us about that, Billy?' Steve said. Billy nearly always felt irritated by his older, more confident cousin, but underneath the brash exterior he knew Steve was a shrewd businessman and a good farmer. Most of the time he seemed at pains to hide it and spent his time flirting with girls or playing practical jokes with his friends. Billy had noticed the way he had kissed Kim under the mistletoe and in his opinion he had held her far longer than was necessary. He had liked the feel of her soft full lips himself and he would have liked to hold her longer too. He had seen her colour rise when he met her eyes but she hadn't blushed with Steve. Did that mean he mattered to her?

'How do these robots do the milking anyway?' his Uncle Struan asked curiously. 'Are they like mechanical men going round the cubicles? And how do they decide when a cow needs milking?'

'N–no, nothing like that.' Billy stifled a laugh at the picture his uncle conjured up of wee metal men shuffling round the cubicle shed amongst the cows. 'The robots are fixed and have to be installed so they're accessible to the cows, and not too far from the dairy. The milk is piped automatically into the bulk tank. The cows come to the robots themselves whenever they feel ready to be milked. Each cow wears a collar which is recognized electronically and every cow is programmed into the computer so that the right amount of cake can be measured out to her each time she is milked. It is more natural because they can be milked several times in twenty-four hours, the way a calf would suckle. The amount of milk and the cake used are all recorded and you can look them up on the computer. It can be linked to the house so you can keep an eye on things easily. Of course there are some problems but it's a lot easier than having to be there for the whole milking twice every day, and you don't need to start at five in the morning.' He glanced at his father.

'I know, I know, I've heard it all before,' Sam said with a sigh.

'It sounds a good system, the way you describe it, Billy,' Alex agreed, 'but what if a cow develops mastitis, or if one is newly calved and the milk cannot go into the bulk milk tank?'

'Yes, I wondered that?' Struan remarked.

'Now, Struan,' Tania interrupted, shaking her head and making a face at Rosemary and Ellen, 'the subject is banned. We're here to celebrate Christmas, remember?'

'Oh but Aunt Tania, just let me tell them this bit,

then we'll forget about farming for today.' Before Tania could agree or disagree, Billy turned to Struan and went on, 'That's one of the reasons the robots would suit me so well. I wouldn't need to carry buckets of colostrum up the steps from the milking parlour pit, nor any milk that has to be kept separate if a cow has been treated with antibiotics. You set the computer and the robot diverts the milk into dump buckets so it doesn't go near the main milk tank.'

'Is that right? It sounds too good to be true.'

'He makes it sound good, doesn't he?' Sam said drily. 'Perhaps he should be a robot salesman instead of farming Martinwold.'

'Oh, Dad! Don't be like that,' Billy pleaded.

'Well, you admitted the robot alerts you on your mobile when the tubes get twisted or something else goes wrong, even if it's in the middle of the night.'

'Trust Dad to remember the bad bits,' Billy chuckled and gave an exaggerated sigh.

'Anyone for Christmas dinner?' Ellen interrupted with a smile and was greeted with a chorus of eager assent.

It was indeed a happy day. Ellen had been diffident about asking Alex's family to Bengairney, knowing what excellent cooks Tania and Rosemary were.

'It's been just like old times,' Sam said, 'With all of us back at Bengairney. You've made our old home look well, Ellen. And Alex is like a new man.' He kissed her cheek warmly as they left. Alex told her how proud he was when they had all gone.

'I never thought I'd have a wife and family of my own and be able to ask them all back here,' he said. 'They all enjoyed the day.'

'Actually, so did I, once I'd served the Christmas dinner and everyone cleared their plates,' Ellen admitted. 'Kim was a great help. I think she enjoyed having your nephews and niece for company.'

'Yes,' Alex agreed, 'I noticed Steve and Billy made the most of the mistletoe, and Billy snatched another chance when they were leaving. I reckon he thought nobody would see but I saw them in the hall mirror.'

'He's a handsome lad. There's no wonder Kim has a crush on him,' Ellen said. 'I hope she doesn't get hurt though. I have a feeling the Lennox girl has her eye on Billy and she would make a good wife for him when she has her veterinary training.'

'Only time will tell,' Alex sighed. 'Whatever they do, I hope neither of them waste as much time as we did.' His voice grew husky. 'I don't intend to waste any more though,' he whispered, drawing her closer.

In the end Alex and Ellen decided they could not manage the holiday with Sam and Rosemary so this would be the first time the two of them had been on a proper holiday alone since their honeymoon, with no family, no cattle sales to attend en route, no other farms to visit.

'We both love our home and our way of life but this will be a brand new experience, going on a cruise down the Rhine,' Rosemary chuckled. 'How will you survive, Sam, without a cow in sight?'

'We shall probably appreciate what we have all the more when we return. I'm sure I shall survive, but will Billy?'

'Sam, he's a man now and he has chosen farming as his work, as his life. We can't worry about him forever and we shall only be away for ten days. If you feel like this now how will you control your worries when we go to Australia for six whole weeks?'

'Mmm, I've been pondering that question. I think you'll have to visit Carol on your own, Rosie,' Sam said.

'Oh no! Carol thinks the world of you, Sam, and she's your daughter just as much as Billy is your son. I've promised we will go at the end of the year. She knows this cruise is a trial to see how Billy copes on his own, and how you feel being torn away from your beloved Martinwold and your cattle. She's already planning and looking forward to us going. Besides I think Alex will keep a discreet eye on Billy, phone him up and so on, and probably pop in some days.'

'Yes, they do get on well, too well sometimes, it seems to me,' Sam said darkly. 'I reckon Alex encourages him over the robots.'

'Mmm, I've noticed he seems quite interested but he says it's not worth his while making the changes at Bengairney and spending so much money when he has no son to follow on.'

'He has Kim now. She's as interested in the breeding side of the herd as Alex is himself.'

'That's different. Kim might marry someone with no interest in farming, then where would Alex be? No, I can understand why he doesn't want to make such major changes himself.'

'I suppose you're right, Rosie. You usually are,' Sam said with a wry smile, 'but I'm still not sure about going off to Australia and leaving Billy entirely on his own for so long.'

'He's looking forward to the challenge and I'm sure

Ellen will invite him for meals now and then.'

'Aye, but it's not his meals I'm worried about. Suppose he had a fall or an accident?'

'That could happen to anyone. Billy always has his mobile phone with him. I never thought I would admit what a useful thing that is, but it does reassure me when he's working in the fields. The doctor says he has adjusted well. It is up to us to accept things the way they are and treat him as any normal young man, instead of keep reminding him of his amputation.'

'That's easier said than done,' Sam muttered.

'He has been so determined to prove he can do nearly everything you can do. Look at the way he insisted on taking his turn at the milking even when he was at university, and he has kept up with all the pedigrees.'

'It's a different thing being in sole charge every day without a break,' Sam said. He heaved a sigh. 'Then there's another thing, and it's a problem Alex doesn't consider because he has never had children of his own, but we have three. Billy can't have everything. I know Rena is more than happy with her share since you signed over Langton Gardens to her, and she has the rents from the houses you owned. She's told me often that she's happy with the way her life is turning out, but Carol has had nothing much yet. Is it fair that she should have to wait until we die before she can have her share?'

'Well, ye–es, there is that,' Rosie agreed slowly. 'I've thought about it myself. Carol was so homesick, especially after Angus was born. I wondered how things would work out then. If she had had money of her own she might have been tempted to come back to Scotland at that time, but she seems happy now. After all, it was love at first sight with her and Paddy and his family welcomed her so warmly. They seem to be quite well off.'

'That's not the same as her having some money of her own,' Sam insisted, 'but we shall see for ourselves how things really are when we visit. If there are any decisions to be made we'll make them when we return. At least Carol has provided us with a grandson, even if it does look as though he'll grow up a wee Aussie. I can't help wondering whether Billy will ever find a wife. I used to think he and Fenella Lennox....'

'Sam Caraford!' Rosemary said in angry exasperation. 'There you go again, belittling our son! Why shouldn't Billy get a wife? He's only lost half a leg, for goodness' sake. He's not paralyzed from the waist down as he could so easily have been. He's good-looking and intelligent and he works as hard as anyone else. Why shouldn't some girl love him for the fine young man he is, and provide you with more grandsons than you might desire?'

Why indeed? Billy thought bitterly, overhearing the latter part of his parents' conversation. He crept silently outside again. Obviously his mother was prejudiced in his favour because he was her son and she loved him unconditionally, but his father had always been a realist and called a spade a spade. He knew well enough that a stump of a leg would be enough to put off lots of girls, irrespective of what he did for a living.

ELEVEN

Billy had looked forward to being left in charge when his parents went on their cruise. He was determined to prove to his father that he could manage everything perfectly well, so he was surprised to find himself feeling depressed at yet another evening preparing and eating his meal alone in the silence of the old house. It didn't seem the same without his mother's cheerful presence and his father either teasing or having some sort of discussion. Common sense told him his mood had nothing to do with the loss of his leg, but he blamed it anyway. He might have gone out and met old friends he had known at school, or through the Young Farmers' Club. Even Michael Appleby was rarely home for long these days. There was no point in going to Gino's. There were younger students there now. He could have called at the pub for a drink and a chat, but he had never wanted to drink the night away, and most of the occupants would be older than him, probably married men with families, escaping the bedtime ritual.

The truth was, if he was honest with himself, he

didn't really know what he wanted. The previous evening he had gone round to Bengairney after his evening meal. He had had an interesting discussion with Uncle Alex about the progeny of a new bull he was trying and Aunt Ellen had insisted on feeding him tea and sandwiches before he left, but he had still felt vaguely dissatisfied. Kim had been out for the evening with some of her college friends because they would soon be finishing their course and going their separate ways. It was only when he arrived home that Billy realized he was disappointed because he had had to leave without seeing her.

Tonight it was a lovely May evening and he might have enjoyed a walk through the woods, or around the fields, for he enjoyed all aspects of nature, but he had been fencing and on his feet most of the day. His arms ached from straining the wires and his thighs throbbed with the effort to maintain his balance while he worked. It was one of the problems he was continually coming to terms with and he had been determined not to find himself sprawling on the ground in front of Jim Sharpe, their general worker. He was a dour bugger at any time and especially when there was work to be done. Billy sensed the older man was something of a sadist as well as lazy. He was just considering removing his prosthesis and stretching out on the settee while he flicked through the television channels when he heard a car drawing into the farmyard. He sighed. Who can that be? he wondered without enthusiasm. If it was Uncle Alex he would come straight in. Anyone else could go away, he decided morosely.

'Hello, can I come in?' Kim's voice called diffidently.

Billy jumped in surprise and swung his legs to the floor as she popped her head around the door of the little sitting room. Billy immediately clicked off the television. 'I don't want to disturb you if you're watching a programme,' Kim said.

'No, no, I'm not. Come in, Kim. I thought you would be too tired for visiting after burning the midnight oil last night.'

'I was not that late! It was not long after eleven o'clock and Aunt Ellen said I'd only just missed you. She has been baking today so she's sent you a rhubarb tart. I left it on the kitchen table.'

'Thanks. I love rhubarb. That must be the first of the season, is it?'

'Yes, it is. Aunt Ellen says you should eat it soon in case the juice makes it soggy but she did put a sprinkling of cornflour in with the fruit to thicken it a little so it should be all right.'

'It will be lovely. We'll try a slice later with some tea, shall we?'

'We–ell, only if I'm not disturbing you?'

'Since when did that bother you, Kim?' Billy cocked an eyebrow at her, but she was looking serious tonight and a bit nervous. He wondered why. 'You're not disturbing me. I could use some cheerful company. I've been fencing most of the day and Jim Sharpe was a grumpy old sod.' His mouth tightened. He was well aware that the man took advantage when his father was away. Moreover he did his best to provoke him and draw attention to his artificial leg, and any tasks he couldn't do as well as other men. 'So tell me about your evening out. Are you finished your final exams now? Was it a celebration? Did you enjoy it?'

'No, not quite, and no, not really, and no, I didn't enjoy it.' She frowned and lowered her eyelashes so he couldn't see the misery in them. Most of the other students were at least a year older than Kim and a few were having a second attempt at education and already in their twenties. They seemed so sophisticated, or at least experienced with life. They had made Kim feel gauche, almost stupid, when they were all gathered together, especially after some of them had a few drinks, yet she knew she was more intelligent than most of them and far more likely to pass her finals with excellent results. Billy frowned at her downcast head. He reached out and stroked the golden tresses of her ponytail. She still wore it fairly long and it was beautifully thick and silky. Billy had admired it from the first time he had seen her.

'Uncle Alex and Aunt Ellen are really proud of you, Kim. Aunt Ellen was saying some of your lecturers think you should go further, maybe do your doctorate in economics.'

'Oh, the study side has been fine,' Kim said, brushing exams aside. 'Except that I've had enough. I'm ready to apply what I have learned and get on with life. Besides, both Aunt Ellen and Uncle Alex are looking forward to me being able to relieve them of some of their paperwork.'

'So? What's the matter then, wee Kim? Are you just tired after your late night?'

'I told you I wasn't late! In fact I was the first to leave, if you must know.' The colour flared in her cheeks as she remembered the laughter as she had left the room where they had moved to after enjoying their meal. All they wanted was to indulge in a good supply of alcohol. Billy frowned, watching her.

'What's bothering you, Kim?' he asked softly. 'You'd better tell me, hadn't you?'

'I–I don't know.' He saw the glimmer of tears in her lovely eyes before she turned hastily away again.

'Of course you must tell me. Whatever it is, it can't be that bad. Can it?' He hesitated at her troubled expression and his frown deepened. 'Even if you're ... I mean, it's not the end of the world if you've.... Well, you have an excuse when you have no mother, or even a sister to – to advise. You know we all love you. We'll stand by you. Come on, tell me, Kim?'

'Even if I've what?' Kim asked sharply, turning to stare at him, blinking away the shimmer of tears.

'Well, it does happen,' Billy said awkwardly. 'Lots of girls do get pregnant and....'

'No! That's certainly not the trouble! You d–don't understand either.' She bit back a sob and when Billy would have drawn her closer she shrugged him away, but Billy was already giving a sigh of relief. Then he wondered why it should matter so much to him. But it did. It mattered a lot. He reached for her and drew her firmly into the circle of his arm.

'Nothing else matters then. I mean nothing else can be as big a problem as expecting a baby before you're ready for one, and especially if you don't love the father.'

'It feels as bad to me. They all laughed and made fun,' she said bitterly, 'then – then t–two of the men made h–horrid suggestions.'

'Kim, my wee sweetheart, I don't know what you're talking about. Start again and tell me what's bothering you and who made you so unhappy. I've never seen you like this before.'

'You promise you'll not laugh too?' she asked, half angrily, half diffidently.

Billy eyed her steadily and nodded.

'I promise.'

'And – and you'll help me?' The colour flared again in her fair skin. She looked lovely, Billy thought, and there was not a grain of vanity in her.

'You know I will help if I can. That's what friends are for, and we've always been friends, haven't we?'

'Yes, I–I think so. I do hope so,' Kim said fervently.

'So what was so terrible and why did they laugh? Did they want to get you drunk, or....' He frowned. 'They weren't trying to persuade you to take drugs, were they?'

'No. Although I'm pretty sure two of them do use drugs, but they've never offered any to me. They know how I feel about such things. I know they think I'm a – a prude. Even the girls on my course, the ones I thought were friends, were laughing and making fun last night. They – they wanted to know who – who I am saving myself for.' She hung her head miserably. 'Even Mary Appleby has tried it,' she muttered, staring at the floor. 'She – she didn't like it, and she wished she hadn't done it, b–but at least she's not a – not a....'

'Not a what?' Billy couldn't imagine what she was talking about and it was not like Kim to talk in riddles. She was always so articulate – straight and to the point.

'A virgin,' she croaked, in little more than a whisper.

'A....' Billy opened his mouth, then closed it again quickly. He had almost laughed aloud but the sight of Kim's face told him this was really upsetting her and she was near to tears. It was totally unlike the mature, sensible Kim he knew and he guessed her companions of the previous evening had teased her cruelly, even if they had not all meant to make her feel so inadequate and miserable. As the full implication of her announcement sank in, Billy's spirits soared, though why that should be he had no idea. He seized her and hugged her tightly. 'My God, Kim, that's not something to be ashamed of. It's something to be proud of. I'm glad you have stuck to your own principles!'

'You are?' She gave a puzzled frown, leaned back a little and stared up into his face to make sure he was telling the truth, and not making fun of her, as they had last night. 'You really mean that, Billy?'

'I certainly do. It's not as though you're one of the ugly sisters, Kim. You're a very attractive girl and I've no doubt you've had plenty of offers, so....'

'But not from anyone I could – could ...' she stammered. 'Two of the men last night were sure they could persuade me to – to....' She shuddered, and cuddled closer against his chest. 'One of them is married.' Billy's arms tightened instinctively. He became aware of her soft warmth and felt his own desire stir. He summoned all his self–control. That was one complication he dare not risk. 'I c–couldn't do it with – with just anybody. But I know you so well and....'

'Aah!' Billy released her and sat up straight, his brow darkening. 'Are you another one who thinks I should be glad of any offer because I've only one leg, or that I shall be different to other men, Kim?' he asked angrily.

Kim stared at him, then blinked.

'I–I don't understand. I–I mean, that doesn't make any difference to a man, does it? I – I know how important good legs are for a bull or a ram. Uncle Alex is always saying that, b–but....'

This time Billy did laugh out loud, throwing back his head.

'God, you're priceless, Kim.' He saw her hurt expression and tried to control his humour. 'Good legs and feet are certainly important for four-legged animals. They need them to stand on if they're to be any use for breeding. I didn't mean to laugh. I'm just relieved you don't see me as different on account of only having one leg, unless you think I should be grateful and seize any offer?' He scowled. 'I know some women might be repelled by the sight of my stump in bed, but it doesn't mean....'

'I don't know what you're talking about, Billy,' Kim interrupted with a frown. 'I can't see why it should matter because you've got Charlie instead of a leg.' She rubbed his knee.

'It's ages since we went swimming together,' Billy said out of the blue, remembering that his stump had never troubled Kim. He felt his spirits rise, but he also experienced a fierce urge to protect Kim from her jeering companions of the previous evening, and others like them.

'Are you on the pill, Kim?'

'No.' She flushed unhappily. 'The girls are always saying I ought to be but they take it in case they go out for the evening and end up having sex and they don't want to get pregnant. I would need to trust a person, and know him well, and I would have to like him – like him a lot. That's why I thought you would help me. There's other things besides the pill. Couldn't you use them?'

Understanding dawned then and Billy's eyes widened, then softened.

'I could, but I'm not going to, Kim. At least not tonight. But make no mistake, I'm certainly tempted,' he added quickly, seeing the look of rejection on her expressive face, 'but you know as well as I do that if Uncle Alex discovered I'd been playing around with you, or if he thought I'd treated you badly, Kim, he would never speak to me, or allow me through his door again. Apart from that I have far too much respect for you.' He sighed. 'You're so intelligent and mature the way you handle things that matter in life, and yet I see now you're so young and innocent in some respects. Uncle Alex and Aunt Ellen have sheltered you from the real world when they allowed you to live at home to finish your education.'

'I'm eighteen!' Kim reminded him indignantly. 'Most of the girls I know have been having sex since they were fourteen or fifteen, at least if what they say is true.'

'I'm not talking about having sex, Kim. Believe it or not there are a lot of men who don't expect it just because they have taken a girl out for the evening, and I'm one of them.'

'You're saying you don't fancy me enough to help me,' Kim said flatly and made to rise, but Billy grabbed her arm and pulled her down again.

'You don't need help from anyone, Kim. It's the greatest gift a girl can offer a man to know you have waited and saved yourself for him and I'd count myself very honoured if you still choose me six months from now.'

'Six months?'

'Yes, six months, and meanwhile I want you to promise you'll not have sex with anyone unless you love him, certainly not just for the sake of experimenting.'

'Oh.'

'Don't say it like that, Kim. Now I know you're ready for the grown-up world, what I would like to do is take you out as my girlfriend. I want us to be seen on dates together. I need to be sure you would not be ashamed to introduce me to your friends or to be seen in public with a hopalong man.' Kim heard the faint bitterness in his voice and even a thread of uncertainty.

'Oh Billy, I'd never be ashamed of you. I'd be proud if you were my companion.'

'Companion, eh? Mmm, well, we'll see. Anyway we need to make Uncle Alex and Aunt Ellen realize you're no longer a child, and that you have a mind of your own. They will probably object,' he warned. 'I need to know whether they disapprove of me personally, or the fact that you're venturing into the adult world and I'm encouraging you.'

'You really mean that, Billy? We'll go out together, just the two of us?'

'Of course just the two of us.' He grinned and kissed her cheek, but Kim flung her arms around his neck and hugged him.

'I knew you'd make me feel better,' she said, 'even though you haven't done as I asked.'

'Don't tempt me further,' Billy growled, fully aware of her full soft breasts pressed against his chest. 'I'm only human, and I've wanted to take you out for a long time.'

'Have you? Truly?' Kim asked incredulously, leaning back to look into his face. Her mouth was temptingly close to his. 'So you're not doing this as a compromise because of – of....'

'No,' he groaned softly and kissed her fully on her parted lips. It was their first real kiss and Billy was astonished at the passion which flared between them. He pressed her closer, moulding her pliable young body to his. She felt his desire but she did not draw away and it was left to Billy to summon his willpower and draw back. He was breathing hard.

'If you tempt me like that too often six months will seem like a lifetime,' he murmured gruffly against her ear lobe. 'Now shall we make that tea and a slice of rhubarb tart?'

'I'll make it,' Kim said, smiling dreamily at him, 'but only if you promise to give me a proper kiss goodnight before I leave, like a proper courting couple.'

'I wouldn't let you away without now that I've had a sample of your kisses, Miss Kimberley Wilshaw,' Billy said with a grin, but inwardly he knew Kim had kindled emotions which had smouldered for some time when he was with her. 'How about going to the swimming baths tomorrow evening? Then we'll see what films are on at the cinema at the weekend. If there's nothing we fancy locally we could drive down to Carlisle.'

'Super.' Kim gave a little skip of happiness as she went into the kitchen.

Neither Sam nor Rosemary seemed to notice that Billy was taking Kim out on a regular basis, or that their friendship was deepening into something more serious than friendship between cousins. They had thoroughly enjoyed their holiday together and returned in high spirits. Sam still flatly refused to consider installing milk robots and Billy was bitterly disappointed. He had hoped they might have had them installed before his parents went to Australia at the year end.

'One thing I do agree with you about, though, is Jim Sharpe,' Sam said. 'He'll have to go. The other men complain that he wriggles out of the work at every opportunity. On top of that too many of our small tools have been going missing.'

'But we marked them all with our initial and postcode using that invisible marker the police recommended.'

'Yes, I know. They've been doing a few checks at the Saturday market in the town and some of our tools have turned up. Apparently the stallholder had bought them cheaply from Jim Sharpe so I don't think we shall have a problem when we give him notice to leave.'

'Well, I can't say I shall be sorry to see him go,' Billy said bitterly. 'He reminds me about my leg, and the jobs I can't manage, at every opportunity.'

The following week Ellen and Alex came over to Martinwold for Sunday lunch and to see the holiday photographs.

'Billy said he would be back in time to join us for lunch,' Rosemary said. 'He seems to have taken up swimming again, but I'm sure it must be good for him. Is Kim not with you?' Ellen and Alex looked at each other with raised brows.

'No, she's swimming too. With Billy. I expect they'll return together. Billy picked her up earlier. Did you see that piece in the paper about the man losing his licence due to dangerous driving? Kim says that's the same man who knocked her off the road that time when it was snowing then shot off without so much as a thank you after Sam towed him out.'

'Is that the same one?' Sam asked. 'One of the other drivers noted his number plate. He was going to mention it to the police. Maybe they have been keeping an eye on him.'

'Yes, but it was not his first offence apparently, or so it said in the paper,' Ellen remarked.

'I didn't see that,' Rosemary said, 'I was too busy reading about Kim. That is a lovely photo of her in the local paper as best student on her course. She seems to have won several other awards as well. Is she sure she doesn't want to go on studying?'

'Yes, she's quite sure,' Alex said, almost defensively. 'You of all people should understand that, Rosemary. You had the ability but you didn't want to spend years at university.'

'That's true,' Rosemary admitted ruefully, 'and what arguments I caused with my mother. So what is Kim going to do?'

'I could employ her full-time,' Ellen said. 'She's always been interested in history and she absorbs everything I tell her about antiques. I don't think she realizes how much that helps when she's talking to customers. They nearly always end up buying from her. Last week she finished off the auctioneering of the porcelain pieces for me because I was losing my voice. Her potted history of each piece was spot on. I am really proud of her, and Trevor would have been too. But Alex is claiming her for two days a week to help him.'

'She'll probably end up getting married anyway,' Alex said, 'so we may as well enjoy her company while we can.'

'She's just a lassie yet,' Sam said. 'A pretty one, though, I must admit.'

'Mmm, well, Billy seems to agree with you about that anyway,' Alex said, with a wink at Ellen. 'At least he's been seeing her at every opportunity since she finished her studies.'

'Billy? So that's where he's been going in the evenings?' Rosemary remarked. 'He's certainly demanding plenty of clean shirts and jeans and I saw he had bought himself a lovely blue cashmere sweater.'

'Och, Kim's far too young to be serious, especially about Billy,' Sam said. 'They have always got on well together.' He looked at Alex. 'We worry that the loss of his leg will make things difficult for him when it comes to finding a suitable wife.'

'Well, Kim is a lot happier than she's been for the past year and they seem to be spending all their spare time together,' Alex reflected amiably.

'Aren't you going to put a stop to it?' Sam asked. 'Kim's far too young.'

'She's eighteen and she's sensible,' Ellen said. 'It's early days yet and she might have lots of boyfriends but Alex and I wish we had met years ago and not wasted so much of our lives. If Kim wanted to settle down with Billy, or another nice young man, we wouldn't object, would we, Alex?'

'It would please me greatly if it was somebody as interested in dairy farming as Billy is.'

'That's what you think,' Sam said darkly. 'You'd soon change your tune if he nagged you to spend more money than you can afford on robot milkers.'

'Oh, I don't know,' Alex mused. 'I've listened to what he says and I've been giving them some consideration. Ellen and I have a lot of time to make up. I don't intend to spend my life working all the hours God sends like I used to do.' He smiled warmly at his wife and Ellen nodded.

'We're agreed on that. We would like to enjoy each other's company now.'

'Mmm,' Sam muttered, 'I'm not ready to sit back and take things easy yet but Billy thinks he's ready to take over and he's forever wanting to make changes.'

'Just like we did when we were young,' Alex reminded him. 'Remember how frustrated we got when we thought Father was going to turn down the opportunity to buy Martinwold?'

'That was different,' Sam said shortly. 'It was a good investment. Anyway,' he said, deciding it was better to change the subject, 'I'll get some glasses from the kitchen and we'll have a drink while we wait for the youngsters to return.'

'Yes, I'd better make sure the meat is not burning too,' Rosemary said, following him into the kitchen. They both stopped in their tracks. Billy had just got out of his car and moved round to open the passenger door for Kim. Her hair was loose and still slightly damp after the swimming. She was tall but Billy was taller and she looked up at him with a smile. He slipped a hand under her hair, lifting it slightly and drawing her closer as he bent to exchange a long slow kiss.

'Well! There's nothing childlike or innocent about

that!' Sam said. 'Surely Kim is far too young? She can't possibly know her own mind yet. I'd hate to see Billy getting hurt.'

'Oh, I'm not so sure,' Rosemary said with a reminiscent smile. 'I knew who I wanted to marry when I was Kim's age.' She glanced up at Sam. He put an arm around her shoulders and hugged her. 'We were married by the time I was twenty-one, remember?'

'So we were,' he murmured, 'and it seems like yesterday. I've never had any regrets, have you, sweetheart?' He kissed her affectionately.

'Not one. I think we should leave Billy and Kim to make their own decisions. They have both had serious problems in their young lives and coping with them has made them stronger and more mature than many at their age. I'd be happy if Billy had a nice girl like Kim for a wife.'

'Where have the years gone?' Sam asked with a sigh. 'He'll need somewhere to live if he gets married. I'm not ready to retire yet. It's easy for Alex to talk but he hasn't got a son nipping at his heels to move him on.'

'I know you're not ready to retire. It's taken enough effort persuading you to arrange our visit to Carol in Australia. At least I shall know Billy will not be lonely while we're away, especially over Christmas.'

'Och, Billy and Kim might be all over by then. You know what young folks are like.'

'Yes, they're the same as we were at their age. The pair of them look so happy,' Rosemary added with a sigh. 'I can't help but wish them well.'

TWELVE

Sam found it hard to accept that his youngest offspring was now a man in his own right. It amazed him that Billy's relationship with Kim seemed to be going from strength to strength, spending most of their spare time together.

'If this goes on we shall have to see about doing up one of the cottages for them to live in when we get back from Australia,' Sam said. 'I'm not ready to move out of Martinwold for a while yet, and while I'm here there will be no milk robots,' he declared for the umpteenth time.

Rosemary sighed.

'So you keep saying, dear.'

'Well, there's no need for Billy to be so bloody independent. He could leave the buckets of colostrum in the milking parlour for someone else to carry out and feed the young calves. He insists on trying to do everything himself.'

'He wants to prove he is as capable as other men. Even when he was a boy you used to tell him he had to learn how to do all the jobs about the farm or he would be no use as a boss if he couldn't show his men how to do things properly.'

'But things are different for him now. He admits losing a leg has made a difference to his balance if he has to carry things.'

'I know, Sam,' Rosie sighed. 'But he's young and determined. Give him time.'

'I'm trying but it doesn't help when my own brother agrees with him about the robots, even if he is considering them for a different reason.'

'I know Alex is convinced the cows will give higher yields if they can be milked several times a day when their udders are full. You must admit it does seem more like nature intended.'

'So he keeps saying,' Sam said glumly, 'but Alex has always concentrated on yields and breeding. We're more commercial at Martinwold. I've noticed he's always keen to go with Billy trekking down into England to see the latest robot installation.'

'But you enjoy going with them and seeing other farms and the way other people do things, don't you, Sam?' Rosemary asked. She longed for her husband and son to agree about future policies, and Alex too. She had known Alex all her life. They were the same age and they had been at school together. They had been the best of friends in those days. But she knew how hard Sam had worked to make a success of Martinwold, first to pay off the bank loan when his father bought the farm, and then to pay out Alex's share so that he was the sole owner. He had done that for Billy's future, but neither of them were ready to hand over yet. Sam was only fifty-one and as fit as many younger men. She sighed. 'Maybe six weeks in

Australia will make you see things differently, Sam.'

'I doubt that. I reckon I shall be ready to come home after the first week.' He grinned at her to show he was only partly serious. He was looking forward to seeing Carol again and they had never seen their eight-year-old grandson, except on Skype and that was not the same. The preparations were all made and Sam and Rosemary would leave home on 14 December. Ellen called at Martinwold to see them.

'Since you will be away for Christmas,' she said, 'I thought we might have an early celebration the Sunday before you leave. Kim and I will do the cooking and have it at Bengairney. We'll invite Tania and Struan. What do you think?'

'I think it's a splendid idea,' Sam said, hearing the end of the conversation. 'Rosemary is like a cat on hot bricks wondering if she has got everything packed and left enough food in the freezer for Billy, and washed everything that moves.'

'He's exaggerating,' Rosemary said with a laugh, 'but I do feel excited, and a bit nervous, now the time has come to go. We've never been away so long before and it's such a long way.'

It was a happy family gathering the following Sunday. Between them Ellen and Kim had made a delicious meal and everyone was happily replete when Billy got to his feet and tapped his glass with a teaspoon.

'Kim and I have some news we want to share with you all before Mum and Dad fly off to Australia. We hope you will wish us well. We have decided to get engaged.'

'Engaged?' Sam echoed incredulously. 'But you

haven't had time to get to know each other. I–I mean....'

Cousin Steve chuckled.

'Come on, Uncle Sam, they've known each other since they were in nappies – well, maybe not that long, but for years anyway. I could see they were attracted last Christmas when Billy made the most of the mistletoe and Kim obviously enjoyed it.'

Sam looked at his nephew, opened his mouth, and closed it again.

'Well, I'm very happy for you both,' Rosemary said and came round the table to give each of them a hug and a kiss.

'Aye, and so are we, aren't we, Ellen?' Alex announced, smiling from ear to ear.

'We are indeed. We wouldn't recommend waiting as long as we did.'

'Did you two know about this?' Sam asked almost accusingly.

'We didn't know about the engagement,' Alex said, 'but it's a pleasant surprise.'

'We're not planning to get married for a year or maybe eighteen months, but we thought – at least I thought, this would convince you we are serious, Dad, and that we're old enough to know our own minds.'

'I see,' Sam said slowly. 'It seems we shall have to make some changes.'

'There'll be time enough for that when you come back from seeing Carol,' Alex said gently, seeing the shock on his older brother's face. He knew Sam was not ready to accept his son was a man and impatient to make his mark in life. He glanced across at Kim. She looked radiantly happy and he vowed he would do all in his power to help the young couple face the hurdles which lay ahead. They were the nearest he would ever have to children of his own and he loved them both.

Later the young folks gathered in Bengairney's small sitting room where their parents had once played as children. Ellen, Rosemary and Tania lingered in the kitchen, chatting and discussing the engagement as they cleared the dishes together.

'Do you fancy walking off your dinner with a look around the cows, Sam?' asked Alex.

'Aye, good idea.' Sam pushed back his chair and followed his brother outside.

'You don't know how lucky you are to have Billy keeping an eye on everything while you're away,' Alex said. 'He might easily have decided to take the easy way out and opt for a desk job when he lost his leg.'

'We're lucky he wasna killed,' Sam agreed with a sigh. 'He's never wanted to do anything but farm. If only he wouldn't keep on about these bloody robots. I'd already spent a fortune extending and modernizing the milking parlour before he had his accident. I guessed he would want to expand and I didn't mind that. It's the way most folk are going, either that or get out of dairying. I'd never have spent the money if I'd known he was going to want robots, except that I don't fancy them myself and I'm not intending to give up for many a year.'

'None of us can see into the future. We just have to make the most of time while we have it. I intend to do that now – with Ellen, of course. She has been invited down to Bristol to do a series of television programmes on antiques in the spring. I knew she was knowledgeable and a good auctioneer in her own field, but I didn't realize she was so well known or that her opinions were highly respected.' Alex sounded bemused.

'I had no idea she was famous,' Sam teased gently. 'Seriously, Alex, that's wonderful news. You must be proud of her, old boy.'

'I am, and not so much of the old, thank you, big brother. The thing is it will be a series so she will have to go down several times to stay. I intend to go with her.'

'You do? And leave the farm? I never thought I'd hear you say you were leaving your precious cows.'

'I admit it will be tough. Nick Fellows is conscientious and a good stockman, but he says himself he never knows when to change the feeding or which bull to use. He can never make a decision without asking me first. You will be back from Australia by then and I wondered whether you would mind if Billy came to oversee things here whenever we're away? If he's willing I'm hoping he might do the relief milking when Nick is off but I wanted to be sure you're agreeable before I ask him. Kim's pretty good too and I reckon she'll help. In fact I think we'd have a job keeping her away.' He grinned.

'I remember Rosie coming to help me before we were married,' Sam mused, 'and her mother played merry hell. Still, it's been a bit of a shock to hear they are so serious.'

'I have to confess I couldn't be more pleased that Kim and Billy will be together. When you come back from Australia we'll have a serious discussion, Sam. I have some suggestions to make but the last thing I want is for us to quarrel again. We were a pair of silly buggers to fall out over the ownership of Martinwold. Billy is the nearest I'll ever have to a son and he's a grand fellow.'

'Aye, I should have trusted you, I see that now, Alex. But you see you have married, after all, and things might have been different.'

'Ellen understands that Bengairney was always our family home and she knows I always intended leaving everything to Billy. She agrees with that. She has her own business and a fine house with it.'

'Well, now that you've told me so much you'll need to tell me what's on your mind, Alex. I promise not to blow your head off. I shall have plenty of time to think over any suggestions while we're in Australia. I shall have a better idea of how finances are with Carol and her husband when I've seen them too. We've never given her any money or property yet, only her wedding and a cheque to cover household things.'

'Aye, I can see you have to play fair with three of them to consider,' Alex said thoughtfully. 'That might be all the more reason to consider my suggestions then. You know I never modernized things here while Bengairney was rented. Things are different now I own it. I'm considering installing robots here after seeing some of the systems we have visited.'

'Could ye afford them, after buying the farm?' Sam asked in surprise.

'Not outright, but I've been looking into the costs. I could lease them for a monthly payment with the option to buy them outright after ten years. Robots are relatively new and there will be a lot of improvements yet, I reckon,' Alex remarked shrewdly. 'So I think this may be the best way to go.'

'I see. Between seeing Kim and your robots, Billy will be spending all his time at Bengairney,' Sam said, half seriously.

Alex gave him a level look and drew a deep breath.

'That's just it,' he said. 'I wouldn't mind if he and Kim settled down here when they get married, especially since you're not ready for him to move into Martinwold.' He held up his hand when Sam began to protest. 'There's a lot of things to discuss, but it would be grand to see Carafords continuing at Bengairney for another fifty years. That would have pleased our parents. There's other considerations for the future though, as well. Kim inherited Highfold Farm from her father. Ellen was going to sell it and keep the money in trust but she decided to hang on and let Kim decide now she's eighteen. It's in my mind that Billy and Kim and myself could form a three-way partnership and farm Bengairney and Highfold land together. The bigger the enterprise the more men we can afford to employ and some day that will be better for Billy, especially when you and I are no longer fit to help him, Sam. I reckon he will be a good manager in a few more years when he's had more experience, especially while he has the two of us to guide him, as our father did for us. As time goes on he will be better without so much physical work, so long as he can afford to employ men to do the manual work.'

'That's true,' Sam mused.

'I'd like to think of Billy and Kim and their bairns continuing the Caraford line at Bengairney. We were all brought up here. It's always been a happy place.'

'Aye, it has,' Sam said slowly, looking round the

familiar farmyard. The old hayloft was still standing where he had found Rosie, all those years ago, half dead with cold and fatigue. 'Aye, there's a lot of memories for all of us here,' he agreed, 'but I'm not sure how a three-way partnership would work out.'

'I need to discuss it with Ellen, of course,' Alex said, 'but so long as I knew my herd was in good hands – as it would be with Kim and Billy – I'd be happy to move out of the house and live at Charmwood. It's a lovely old house and there's plenty of room. We have discussed building on a sunroom at the back if we ever live there. I'd be back every day to work and to see how things were going here. As I said there's a lot to discuss and iron out. Billy may not agree. I wouldn't like to cause any more family rifts.'

'No–o,' Sam said. 'I never expected anything like this, Alex. I'm not sure what Rosie will think about Billy living somewhere else.'

'He'll be doing that anyway when he gets married.'

'That's true. And he'd not be far away if he was here. We'll not mention it to any of them yet, if you don't mind. I'll discuss it with Rosie when we're on the plane to Australia. It will give her something else to think about. As for Billy and Kim, they'd be foolish not to accept such a generous offer, especially when it means they can be together, so I don't see any problem there.'

'Good.' Alex gave a sigh of relief. 'I was half afraid you'd blow up and refuse to consider the idea.'

'It's a generous offer,' Sam said simply, 'but in the end it will have to be Billy's decision, and Kim's.' He smiled. 'She's a lovely lassie. I hope she's sure about the future when she's so young. Although we argue over the robots I'd hate to see Billy hurt. Rosie says she knew her own mind when she was eighteen, in spite of her mother doing her best to come between us.'

'She did too.' Alex grinned. 'I'd have stepped into your shoes like a shot then, if you'd given me half a chance, but I've been lucky in the end, even if I did wait a long time for happiness to come knocking at my door. As I said, Ellen and I mean to make the most of our time together now we have each other. I'd hate to see anything come between Billy and Kim though. I love them both as though they were my own bairns.'

Billy was not surprised when his mother telephoned from Australia to say they had arrived safely and Carol was overjoyed to see them, as was eight-year-old Angus.

'Tell your Uncle Alex we shall send them an email when we get settled but I think he has made a very generous offer. Your father and I have had a long discussion during the journey.'

'What sort of offer?' Billy asked curiously. 'What have you and Dad been discussing?'

'I expect Alex will tell you all about it. It will be up to you and Kim to decide. I must go now. Look after yourself, Billy. Carol sends her love.' The line went dead and Billy stared at it in frustration. What was his mother talking about?

He was busier than he had anticipated without his father and with the winter work. All the animals were inside now and needing to be fed, cleaned and bedded each day. Jim Sharpe had left without notice, but of his own accord. It had been left to Billy to hire a new man just before his parents left for Australia. His name was Hugh Brown and Billy felt he was going to be a reliable man with the stock. He was pleasant and conscientious, almost an exact opposite to the middle-aged moody Jim. He still had a lot to learn about the way things were done at Martinwold, where things were stored, how the rations were made up and mixed for the various classes of stock, especially the dairy cows, but he was keen and willing. He had only been married a year and his wife was expecting their first baby. The farm cottage was their first home together and they were enjoying painting and decorating it. As a result Billy had little time to visit Bengairney and he was happy when Kim called on him every second evening to eat their evening meal together.

'Mum said they had had a big discussion during the journey. Something to do with us and a suggestion from Uncle Alex. I don't know what she was talking about. Have you heard anything, Kim?'

'No, unless it has something to do with Aunt Ellen's trip down south to take part in a television programme about antiques?'

'I can't see what that has to do with us, can you?'

'No, not really.' She looked up at him with a wide smile. 'I shall be staying on my own while they're away so you'll have to come and see me then.'

'I'll certainly do that.' Billy chuckled, giving her a hug and finishing it off with a long kiss. 'Nothing will keep me away. I'm glad Uncle Alex and Aunt Ellen have taken our engagement so well.'

It was Christmas Eve before Billy was at Bengairney for any length of time.

'We've had several emails from your mother, Billy,

but I expect you've heard all the news too?'

'You mean about Carol expecting another baby? Yes, Mum said that. I'd never heard about her having two miscarriages before. Apparently she had planned to go with Paddy on a sailing trip to do some diving while Mum and Dad were there to look after young Angus, but she's not going now. I'm amazed that Dad has agreed to go in her place. I didn't know he was that fond of sailing?'

'Neither did I,' Alex laughed. 'He used to be a good swimmer but I can't imagine him wanting to dive. I believe there's about half a dozen of them going.'

'Mmm, so it seems. What was it Mum and Dad were discussing on the journey out? Mum said you'd be telling me all about it?'

'Aye, I thought I'd better mention my suggestion to Sam first. I didn't want any more family quarrels if he took offence. Of course, I know it will be up to you, and Kim, in the end. After all, Highfold Farm belongs to Kim now that she is eighteen. It will have vacant possession by next May.'

Billy tensed. Kim had never mentioned anything about Highfold to him. He blinked and tried to pay attention as Alex explained his idea for the three-way partnership and installing robots at Bengairney. He had expected his nephew would be thrilled at the prospect but instead Billy was staring at him and his face was dark with anger, just as Alex remembered his own father. In fact, Billy resembled Steven Caraford, his grandfather, in many ways, not least his pride and independence. Billy turned to Kim.

'You never told me that Highfold Farm belongs to you, Kim,' he said accusingly.

'I didn't really know or at least I never thought about it,' she said simply and looked at Ellen for help.

'Bengairney and Highfold were two of the rented farms left after the taxes were paid when my father died. My brother's death meant a second lot of taxes. Anything left after they were paid was Kim's inheritance. As you know, Alex bought Bengairney outright and we sold the Home Farm. That leaves Highfold. It was in trust for Kim until her eighteenth birthday. She can sell it or do what she wishes with it, but surely Alex is right, Billy? It will make a really good unit along with Bengairney and give you sufficient scope to employ decent men and manage the whole enterprise as a single business. It will also let Alex have more time for leisure if you take over.'

Still Billy stared stonily at them all, his mouth tight.

'A three-way partnership!' he snapped. 'Some partnership with my wife supplying one farm, my uncle another, not to mention the famous Bengairney herd. What have I got to add to this so-called partnership? Damn all! My father is a long way off being ready to hand over Martinwold, or anything else.'

'In one of her emails your mother said if you and Kim agreed your father was willing to transfer half the Martinwold herd to your name and for you to move them here, to Bengairney. Sam reckons he could build up the numbers again in three to six years, but he's not sure he wants to keep as many cows when you will not be there to help him.'

'I'm not ungrateful to my father for his offer,' Billy said tightly, 'but it still makes me a – a pauper in this so-called partnership. If you don't mind I don't think I will stay for the meal.' He moved to the door and went out to the car without so much as a goodnight to any of them. He didn't hear Kim call his name in distress. He didn't wait to see her white face, or the way her lovely eyes filled with tears.

It was the most miserable Christmas either Billy or Kim could remember. Kim tried to telephone but Billy was not answering either the house phone or his mobile. She considered going to Martinwold to talk to him.

'Leave him to stew, lassie,' Alex advised unhappily. 'He's an ungrateful young wretch. I should have guessed the Caraford pride might stand in his way. When he's had time to cool off you might point out to him that he'll be supplying the manager's skill as well as a lot of the labour, and if he doesn't make a decent job of it there'll be no profit for any of us.'

Even so, Alex emailed Australia to tell Sam he'd made a pig's ear of his proposal and Billy had walked out on them all and he wanted to wring his neck for making Kim so miserable.

It was Christmas night before Billy thought of sending Christmas greetings to his parents. There was an email from them already waiting for him.

'We tried to telephone to wish you Happy Christmas but it would be breakfast time there and maybe you had not come in,' his mother had written. 'Since then we have had an email from Alex. Your father and I think you should go over and apologize to him, and especially to Kim. It is not her fault she has inherited a farm. One day you will inherit Martinwold. Although you will need to pay Carol part of its value, you will still be a very lucky man. Swallow your stupid pride and grow up, Billy. Kim is a lovely girl and you're letting your own pride stand in the way of happiness.'

Billy read the rest of the email and the general news, including his parents' delight in sharing Christmas with young Angus, but he could not bring himself to reply. They didn't understand how he felt and he wasn't sure whether he and Uncle Alex would agree over everything when it came to working together every day – or at least that was what he told himself as he tossed and turned in bed and couldn't sleep.

Consequently he was deadly tired by the evening of Boxing Day when news came through from Australia that shook him to the core. Carol's husband and another man had died while out on the diving trip and his father was missing, also feared drowned.

THIRTEEN

'I must go to see Billy,' Kim said the moment Alex told her the news. 'He's all alone and he'll be devastated.'

'It's very late,' Ellen said doubtfully. 'But there's no doubt Billy will be in need of comfort,' she added quickly, seeing Kim's lower lip tremble with distress.

'God, this is a terrible thing to happen,' Alex said when they heard Kim's car draw away. 'I can't imagine how Rosemary must be feeling. As for Carol, poor lassie, expecting another baby and with a young son to bring up on her own. Thank God we parted good friends.'

'It certainly puts things into perspective,' Ellen agreed sadly. 'I hope Billy sees things more clearly and seizes his chance of happiness while he can. I'm sure he will have had a most unhappy Christmas. Kim certainly has.'

Billy rubbed his eyes fiercely when he saw the outdoor light come on and Kim's yellow car drawing up at the door. It was a cold night and she ran straight inside and almost literally into his arms. She could feel him trembling and she knew she had done the right thing to come.

'I don't know what to say to comfort you, Billy.' She hugged him tightly and felt him bow his head to rest his cheek against the warmth of her neck. 'I suppose you heard the same as Uncle Alex? He's terribly upset.'

'Aye,' Billy said gruffly. 'It was Mum who phoned. She said the doctor had been and given Carol a mild sedative and said she must rest for the sake of the baby. I can tell she's putting on a brave face for the sake of Carol and wee Angus.'

'She must be feeling as though her own world has turned upside-down but Uncle Alex says she's always been brave in times of trouble. Is the fire on, Billy? Shall we go through to the room?'

'I expect it's nearly out. I–I haven't been able to think straight since Mum phoned.' They went through to the room together and Kim poked the embers into life and put on some of the smaller logs. It was comforting to see the flames dancing up the chimney and she added coal. Billy watched in silence, his face drawn and pale.

'I know you will not be able to sleep much tonight, Billy, so we may as well be warm in here together.'

'I haven't been able to sit still since Mum phoned,' Billy admitted. 'I hope the shock doesn't make Carol lose this baby too. She loves children. She was always good with me when we were young. She meant to be a teacher but it was love at first sight for her and Paddy. They hadn't known each other long but they got married so that she could go back to Australia with him. It's made me think they were right to seize their chance of happiness.'

'Oh Billy, I'm sure they were. I suppose there is no doubt about Paddy being dead?'

'No, they found his body, and the other man. I don't know exactly what happened but I think they had been diving. Mum said something about a shark attack, although they didn't expect sharks where they were going.'

'And your father? Uncle Alex said they hadn't found his – his body?'

'He had been swimming.' He shook his head. 'I can't believe he's dead. Mum said the same. Unless they find his body, I don't know how she will be able to accept it.'

'It must be dreadful, and them being in a strange country and so far away.' Kim couldn't suppress a shiver and Billy's arm tightened, drawing her closer.

'I keep trying not to think about it. I mean, you hear of men being attacked by a shark and never seen again.'

'Did you eat any supper, Billy?'

'No.' He shook his head. 'It didn't seem right. I mean, doing normal things.'

'I know. Aunt Ellen said that's how you would feel. She said she couldn't eat when my father died. They'd always been so close. She said I must see that you eat something because you have to keep up your strength for your mother's sake. She is going to need all your help and support.'

'I suppose so,' Billy said.

'So shall I make us some sandwiches and coffee, or would you like me to cook you some bacon and egg? I'll bring it in here on a tray.'

'Will you have some too?'

'Yes. We couldn't eat our meal either after we got the news, but I'm peckish now and it's such a cold night.'

'All right. It will have to be something tasty then to tempt us.'

'OK, bacon and egg it is then.' Kim set the bacon to cook on the Aga and went upstairs to Billy's room, then changed her mind and went to the spare bedroom where she knew there was a king-size bed with duvet and pillows. She carried them down to the hall. She couldn't leave Billy alone tonight, whatever Aunt Ellen thought of her staying alone with him. She dumped them on the long seat in the hall and went to see to the food.

Half an hour later they both ate with the appetites of the young and energetic.

'You were right, Kim, I do feel better for that.' He lifted the trays and set them aside then he drew her close. 'I'm so sorry I was such an ungrateful bugger the other night. I still can't come to terms with Uncle Alex's suggestion, or the fact that you will own a farm of your own. I still feel I shall be the pauper with nothing to offer.'

'Uncle Alex says you have the most important thing of all to give – your knowledge and your labour, not to mention your youth. He said he wished he was your age again, then he added with a grin "so long as Ellen could be there as well". He say he doesn't know half the stuff about computers that you know, and the robot system is dependent on them.'

Billy was silent for some time, staring into the fire, then he stirred himself.

'Well, I'm truly sorry I hurt you, Kim, walking out the way I did, and being so – so childish, but everything has changed now. I–I don't know what will happen without Dad. I must consider Mother before everything else. There will probably be inheritance taxes to pay on Martinwold.' He pushed his hands through his hair. 'God only knows what will happen, but remember this, Kim, I do love you and I don't want us to throw away our lives because of my stupid pride.'

'That's good then, because I love you too, Billy Caraford. Now I'm going to clear away our dishes while you make us a big bed on the floor in front of the fire. The duvet is in the hall. Now, don't argue because you know you will probably not sleep at all if you go to bed alone.'

When Kim returned from the kitchen she saw that Billy had spread a thick travelling rug on the floor and piled on the pillows and the big duvet. She blushed as she looked from the bed to him. He raised his dark brows in question.

'I understand if you've changed your mind, Kim,' he said softly, 'but I would welcome your company tonight, and I promise not to do anything you don't want me to do. Can you trust me?'

'You know I trust you, Billy,' Kim said simply and knelt beside him on the floor. He drew her gently into the curve of his arm.

'I feel so restless,' he said. 'If Dad is really dead I think I ought to feel it in here.' He tapped his chest with a clenched fist. 'If I could believe it, I think I could accept it, but I can't. Did you feel like that when your father died, Kim?' He leaned up on his elbow and looked down into her face.

'No, but it was different. The hardest part was when I knew he was terminally ill. I couldn't accept it. I wept and raged and – and I even screamed at Aunt Ellen, but she was hurting too. They were twins and they had always been together, and they were business partners too and my father wanted to move back here.' She sighed. 'Looking back I must have made that first week hell for Aunt Ellen but she convinced me that we must be as kind and cheerful as we could so that my father could be happy in our company for all the time he had left. She was right, of course. I think I grew up five years in that one week. It is different in your father's case. He is so far away and if they don't find his body it will be dreadful for your mother. You will have to be strong for her sake, Billy.' As she talked she slipped her hand inside his shirt and stroked his chest soothingly. Her hand moved down to his stomach. Innocent and diffident though she still was, Kim knew with a feminine instinct as old as time that this was the way to comfort Billy and bring him a measure of peace, maybe even a few hours of sleep. She heard him draw in his breath as her hand moved to his thigh. Slowly, gently, he began to undress her, pausing every now and then to kiss her, or to look into her eyes and make sure she still wanted him as much as he wanted, and needed, her. Then they were lost from the real world, exploring a new world of exquisite discovery, together at last.

They were sound asleep in each other's arms when the shrill ring of the telephone in the hall disturbed them. The fire was burning low but Kim could still see her watch.

'It's 2.30 in the morning,' she said, sitting upright. Billy shivered and pulled on his shirt as he strode quickly towards the hall. Kim couldn't hear the conversation but she knew Billy would be cold when he returned. She piled more logs on the fire and some pieces of coal, but she was shivering with nerves and the chill air of the winter night. She pulled on her blouse and sweater but she couldn't lie down again.

'They've found him!' Billy burst into the room. 'A fishing boat picked him up and they have taken him to a hospital some distance away. He's unconscious but he's alive, Kim. Thank God he's alive.'

'Oh Billy, that's wonderful,' Kim breathed, holding out a hand to pull him back under the covers and get warmed while he told her everything he knew.

'It was Mother who phoned. She hasn't seen him yet. The boat had picked him up quite a distance from where their own boat had set out. He was floating on his back and completely exhausted, barely conscious in fact, but they pulled him aboard and wrapped him up then alerted the coastguard to have an ambulance waiting. Mother could hardly speak for relief, but she's desperately worried about Carol. She is going to phone again when they have more news but she says she will feel better when she has seen Dad and spoken to him. Carol's mother-in-law has offered to come and stay with Carol and Angus while Mother travels to the hospital. She wants to stay beside Dad until he can be moved but she says she feels torn between Carol and wee Angus, and Dad needing her.'

'We shall have to tell Uncle Alex,' Kim said. 'He will be so relieved.'

'Yes, I'll phone and tell him. Even though Dad is so

ill, it's such a relief. The doctor at the hospital told Mum he was extremely fit and once they get some fluids into him they expect him to recover completely.' He reached for his mobile and phoned Bengairney while Kim tucked the duvet round him to warm him up.

'Uncle Alex is as relieved as we are,' Billy said, setting aside his phone.

'I can understand how difficult it will be for Aunt Rosemary,' Kim said softly, 'grieving for Carol when she has lost her husband, and yet filled with relief and joy at the news of Uncle Sam.'

'Yes, so can I,' Billy said, snuggling closer, holding her tightly to share each other's warmth. A little while later when they had warmed each other from top to toe, he whispered, 'It will be even better this time, Kim.'

'Yes,' she breathed exultantly. 'Oh yes.' Her passion rose to match his own.

It was the middle of February before Sam and Rosemary arrived back from Australia. Carol and Angus were with them. Carol was finding it difficult to make any decisions but she had agreed to stay at Martinwold until her baby was born. The day after their arrival, Rena came down on her own to see her twin. They were identical except for a birth spot on Carol's neck. They talked and talked. Rosemary left them closeted together, knowing they had always shared their innermost thoughts and she knew it was the best thing for Carol now. She had been too quiet and withdrawn but time with Rena might relieve her tension until she felt ready to make decisions and take up the threads of her life again.

'Leaving them together seemed the most sensible

thing to do,' Rosemary said to Ellen. 'Carol and Rena were always close. But you will understand that, being a twin yourself.'

'Indeed I do. I know nothing will make up for losing her husband but having a loving family around her must be a great comfort. Billy says Angus is a lovely wee boy and he follows his grandfather everywhere.'

'He does. He knows he has to go to school soon but he was used to having a pony at home so Sam has promised to buy him one as soon as he starts school here, to sweeten the pill a little. Once he has settled in I don't think he should have too much trouble. He is a bright boy.'

'Yes, Billy says he's continually asking questions about the cows. I gather he was not used to dairy animals?'

'No, his other grandfather, and his father, had sheep and beef and crops. He's fascinated with the milking parlour. Between his lively company, and the enforced rest, Sam seems to have been rejuvenated. Angus's grandparents have promised to come over to visit after the baby is born. My heart goes out to them. They have a daughter and other grandchildren, but Paddy was their only son. If Carol decides to stay over here Sam is going to apply for planning permission to do up the old dairy cottage. It would give her a measure of privacy and independence but it is only at the other side of the farmsteading so we would be on hand to help and Angus will be able to see the animals and the farm as often as he wants. Farm children are lucky to have so much freedom and so many things to interest them.'

*

Carol gave birth to a baby girl at the end of June and her parents-in-law came over for the christening at the end of August and stayed for six weeks. Before they left, Rosemary had a long talk with them. She was relieved and grateful that they understood Carol's decision to stay in Scotland and make her home at Martinwold.

Ellen's television series had gone well and she had been booked for another series in a year's time, but she had not bargained for the extra trade it had brought to her own fledgling business.

'Alex is a tower of strength,' she confided to Rosemary. 'I don't want the business to get too big and take over my life – not now.' She grinned. 'But he has helped me clear one of the Charmwood barns and do it up so that I can hold auctions there whenever I accumulate too much stuff. He introduced me to the Bailey Brothers. They do local furniture removals; they only have one lorry. They are careful and clean and we have made an arrangement with them to help with any house clearances I take on. They're very obliging when I need to deliver larger items of furniture, or rearrange pieces here at the house for showing the public. Come through and I'll show you the sunroom we have built on. It's almost finished, except the floor.'

'Oh, Ellen! This is lovely,' Rosemary exclaimed with genuine delight. 'And it is private from the two rooms and entrance hall you keep for showrooms, yet it is so convenient for your lovely big kitchen.'

'Yes, we've made a small sitting room upstairs as

well for the winter. It has a good view and it's cosy. I have my office up there and we have three bedrooms so it is all working fine. Best of all is that Alex is looking forward to us moving in here with just the two of us – much as we both love Kim. We realize she and Billy are a younger generation with lives and decisions of their own to make.'

'And Alex is going ahead with installing the robots, I hear, much to Billy's delight and satisfaction.'

'Yes, they should be finished before the wedding but Alex is waiting for Billy and Kim to return from their honeymoon before they start them up.' Ellen smiled conspiratorially. 'I think he's a wee bit afraid he may not understand all the workings, especially the computer connections.'

'Oh, I'm sure he will,' Rosemary said. 'Alex was always intelligent when we were at school together, and he's used computers for years now.'

'Yes, but mainly for accounts and feeding the cows in the parlour. Besides, he wants Billy to know he's needed. He still has a bit of prickly pride because Kim owns Highfold.'

'He'll get over that, I'm sure. He looks so happy when he's with Kim. I never thought I would see him this happy.' Rosemary shuddered, remembering how Billy had looked that first night at the hospital. 'Even Carol is finding some joy in her life again with the two children, and being near enough to see Rena whenever she wants to talk. I feel I am so blessed.'

'Mmm, me too,' Ellen agreed. 'Life is full of ups and downs, isn't it? Kim is going for the final fitting for her wedding dress on Saturday. Mary Appleby is coming down for the weekend to try on her bridesmaid's dress.'

'I'm glad the two of them have stayed friends through the years,' Rosemary said, 'and Michael has agreed to be Billy's best man.'

'Yes, he's a grand young man, and so meticulous,' Ellen said. 'I'm quite sorry he works so far away. He made a good job of clerking for me that time we had the auction at Highfold for Jane Lennox.' She chuckled suddenly. 'Billy got a surprise when we learned the identity of Michael's girlfriend. Mary knew he had one but he had never told them her name, then he asked if we would invite Fenella to the wedding.'

'Yes, I believe Michael and Fenella had kept in touch all through university, even though they were in different places. Apparently friendship blossomed into love, but not even Michael's parents knew her identity. Michael seemed to think Billy regarded Fenella as his special girl and he was reluctant to spoil their own friendship. It must have been a great relief when Billy and Kim announced their engagement and he realized how wrong he had been. It seems Billy had often talked about the Lennox family when he and Michael shared the flat and of course Billy and Fenella used to meet at Gino's when she was down in this area. They often teased each other and reminisced, but Billy has known Fenella since she was in nursery school so of course it was only friendship they shared.'

'Maybe it was, but I suspect Kim wondered if there was more between them. Mary said all the secrets came out after they saw Kim and Billy's engagement in the paper.'

*

Rosemary had made Ellen, Kim and Mary a special appointment with her own hairdresser on the morning of the wedding and they all looked lovely, Mary with her dark hair bouncing on her shoulders in loose waves and Kim with her thick honey-gold hair like a crown on top of her head. Her young face was radiant and Alex was as proud as if she had been his own daughter as he escorted her down the aisle. Billy gasped with admiration when he half turned and saw her coming towards him. Michael smiled.

'She is beautiful indeed,' he whispered.

Everything about the day went well, even the weather. When Kim threw her bouquet over her head it was Mary's partner, a tall, slim young man, who caught it and handed it quickly to Mary with a special smile as he whispered, 'I think it should be our turn next, sweetheart.'

Michael and Fenella showered the bride and groom with confetti.

'Just you wait,' Billy called with a grin. 'We shall get our own back next year when it's your turn.'

It was a month since Kim and Billy had returned from honeymoon. Both Alex and Billy were well pleased with the way the Bengairney cows had taken to the robots and everything was working splendidly.

'I think I've got the best of both worlds,' Alex said. 'I still have my cows and now I have a family to help me and a wife to love me.'

'So you've no regrets about installing the robots?' Billy prompted.

'Not one, laddie. I'd be crazy to want to go back to getting up at five every morning.'

'Billy, I think we should invite your parents to Sunday dinner and you can show your father how well the robots are working,' Kim suggested. 'I will see how I manage the cooking on my own. If all goes well we can invite all the family another time. What do you think?'

'I think I've married the best girl in the world, and I'm the happiest man alive,' Billy replied with a grin before seizing her in his arms and giving her a kiss which left her breathless and flushed.

Kim enjoyed cooking and the meal was excellent. 'It's been lovely to have a delicious meal made for me without having to lift a finger,' Rosemary said as she thanked Kim and kissed her cheek. 'Bengairney has always felt like home to me, even though I was not born here,' she added with a reminiscent smile. 'Sam's parents always made me welcome even when I was a little girl, and now I feel welcomed all over again.'

Sam agreed the cows seemed to have adapted well to the new system and the old place was looking clean and prosperous.

'I think your parents would have loved Kim and Billy living at Bengairney,' Rosemary said as she and Sam drove home together. 'Kim is a young edition of Megan Caraford, the way she makes us welcome. Tania thinks so too. Now Bengairney will be the hub of the Caraford family again.